SECO

Sister Hana Dean had left her post at a London teaching hospital because of an unhappy love affair. So when she clashes with surgeon Jake Carlyon at the Bridgestead Cottage Hospital can her self-respect allow him to drive her back?

SECOND CHANCE AT LOVE

BY
ZARA HOLMAN

MILLS & BOON LIMITED
London · Sydney · Toronto

First published in Great Britain 1983
by Mills & Boon Limited, 15–16 Brook's Mews,
London W1A 1DR

© Zara Holman

Australian copyright 1983
Philippine copyright 1983

ISBN 0 263 74407 8

Set in 10 on 11½ pt Linotron Times
03/0983–57,000

Photoset by Rowland Phototypesetting Ltd
Bury St Edmunds, Suffolk
Made and printed in Great Britain by
Richard Clay (The Chaucer Press) Ltd
Bungay, Suffolk

CHAPTER ONE

Six months ago she wouldn't have been prepared to do this stupid thing. Even three months ago she would have had more sense, she thought miserably as she sought the road sign which would tell her where to turn off the main road for the little village of Clyston. Her awful sinking feeling increased as she realised the place she wanted was a mere six miles away, but she gritted her teeth, slipped into third gear and turned right across the empty carriageway before she had the chance to change her mind.

It was impossible for her to think of anything else now and she worried again at the theme which had been keeping her company since leaving London earlier that morning. Three months ago she would have had more sense than to interfere in someone else's private life, even if it *did* concern one of her nurses. And it wasn't the first time that one of those silly young girls had misjudged a man's intentions. And not just the very young, she remembered with the all too familiar stab of anguish. Only, at twenty-five, you expected people to have learned something of life, to have more sense than to make absolute fools of themselves. As she had done.

It was hard, when you really got down to it, to escape the conclusion that in fighting Kim Barclay's battles for her she was trying to get her own back on men in general and Lindsay Anderson in particular. And just because this John Carlyon of . . . Hana took her eyes briefly from the road to search for the piece of paper Kim had given her . . . of Dene House, Clyston.

5

Perhaps it would be possible for her to leave the package without making any comment. At the time when Kim Barclay, drowning in tears and melodrama, had confessed to Hana the details of the brief affair with this man Hana had been struggling with her own blighted hopes. That and nothing else had made her assume the role of guardian angel, defender of her sex against the faithlessness of men. But now that she had time to think . . .

The village was upon her before she was ready for it, a pretty place with all the charm that made the West Country so attractive. In the centre was a small pond with one or two water hens swimming briskly in and out of a clump of reeds while at the far side a few ducks floated, drowsy in the sun. And specially laid on for any artist who might be passing, under the shade of a delicately green willow sat a small boy, fishing rod drooping in his hand as he reached into his basket for a sandwich.

About the pond and the adjoining village green the road described a vague circle, the houses grouped haphazardly along it in a way that although it owed nothing to town planning was utterly captivating. But Hana, driving round slowly, her eyes searching doors and gates for names, was immune to its attractions, aware only of a steady increase of the tensions within her, tensions which eight years of training were doing little to control. The Lichfield Arms was passed and almost next to it the village shop cum post-office, both dreamily deserted at this time on a Saturday afternoon and no good as a source of information on the whereabouts of Dene House.

Hana sighed in irritation as her circuit began for the second time, then as she saw the boy get up from his position at the side of the water and as he appeared to be the only soul stirring in the entire place she stopped and pulled on the hand brake with a savage little jerk. The close cropped grass was soft under her feet as she crossed towards him and she found herself smiling, partly in an attempt to get a response, partly because at last her attention was caught by the idyllic appeal of the scene.

'Can you tell me where I can find Dene House?'

Speculative dark eyes surveyed her calmly from a brown, healthy, not too clean face. 'Mr Carlyon is it?'

'That's right.' Hana's smile increased when she saw just how closely he was absorbing each detail of her appearance, from the fair hair cascading about her shoulders, the open-neck checked shirt and the sleek pink jeans. He took his time before replying but apparently what he saw met with approval for he smiled slowly before raising one grubby hand to point.

'Top of the village. House on the right.'

'Thanks.' Grateful as much for his admiration as for his concise instructions Hana turned away, feeling his eyes following her till she reached the car and she was unaccountably disappointed that he didn't respond to her wave as she drove away and up the hill. Of course he *had* picked up his basket and his hands were full, but still. It didn't strike her that she must be feeling nervous if she were anxious about such a meaningless gesture. And in any case she knew that already. She was really very nervous.

When she reached the gate the name was there for anyone to see. Twice in fact. Now that she had stopped the car she could see it clearly enough, on each of the rather imposing stone pillars. Not that the house was all that imposing. That at least was a relief, for in spite of what Kim had told her she hadn't been expecting John Carlyon to be a man of property.

But Dene House was more like a lodge. She comforted herself with that thought when she pulled the car onto the grass verge at the side of the road and switched off the engine. She was much less naive than Kim Bradley, less ready to be impressed. She was fairly certain that he would be a very ordinary kind of man. The kind Sister Hana Dean would be more than capable of dealing with. She had met the type too often . . .

Hana had reached into the rear of the car, searching among all her cases and worldly belongings for the cardboard box Kim had given her and was emerging with it in her hand when she heard a step on the gravel and found herself looking at a woman coming out of the drive of Dene House. She was middle-aged, brown as a berry with dark eyes which swept over the visitor's tall figure with no pretence at hiding her curiosity. Hana felt her cheeks grow warm, suddenly longing to thrust her package into the woman's hands and escape without further explanation.

'Is . . . is this Dene House?' In view of the statement emblazoned on the pillars the question was little short of idiotic.

'Yes.' The woman half-smiled as she took a step down the road towards the village, giving the impression of someone torn between natural inquisitiveness and pressing responsibilities. 'Yes, it is.'

'Is Mr Carlyon at home?' Instinctively Hana crossed her fingers, desperately hoping for a negative reply.

'Bless you, yes. He is that. You'll find him at the back, my dear. Tying up roses he is. But now you must excuse me. I've got to hurry back or my Harry will be off to Exeter without me.'

'Mr John Carlyon?' Hana's voice held a note of panic.

'Of course, Mr John Carlyon.' The woman laughed as she walked backwards away from Hana. 'This is where he lives. Just you go round to the end of the house.

You'll find a door in the wall, go through that and you'll find him. Quite pleased he'll be, to have a visit from such a pretty maid on an afternoon.'

'Oh.' There was nothing else to say. Knowing what she did Hana doubted it, but it was pointless to delay the woman who was so intent on getting back to her Harry and Exeter so she crossed the road and began to walk reluctantly up the gravel drive.

Freed from the restrictions of the hedge which formed a roadside boundary Hana found that she had to revise her opinion of the house just a little. It wasn't enormous but it wasn't small either, and it was the fact that it was built in the shape of the letter L which gave the wrong impression to anyone passing on the road. Its large garden had a well tended look with smooth lawns sloping away from the drive towards wide borders of pink roses. Even from a distance their scent reached her and the sound of searching bees was loud in her ears.

The parcel was heavy now, the string cut into her finger as she crunched along, wondering for the umpteenth time that day why she had got herself into this ridiculous situation. Hadn't she problems enough of her own! But there, looming in front of her, impossible to avoid was the stained wood door, set snugly into the faintly crumbly old brick of the wall.

She expected it to screech when she opened it, but instead it swung back smoothly, on oiled hinges, like everything else in this house she thought sourly. There was no doubt about it, Mr John Carlyon had it made. This must be a perfect place for impressing young girls. What could be easier? Drive them down here in a fast car, go out to one of the plushy restaurants which must be common in the neighbourhood, dine them well and wine them. Then back here and the word seduction need never be thought of, the girls would simply throw themselves at you. And she was sure now that Kim Barclay had been only one of many. She didn't imagine that Mr John Carlyon—each time she repeated the name in her mind her anger with him grew—would have any serious intention towards a student nurse who although pretty enough wasn't particularly bright and . . .

Just then Hana, her heart hammering now as much with anger and indignation as with nervousness, caught sight of a figure at the far end of the lovely enclosed garden and he was doing exactly what the woman, the housekeeper or whatever she was, had said. Some roses had apparently disengaged themselves from staples attaching them to the wall and the man perched on a stepladder was tying them up.

Even at that distance and in that position there was something impressive about him. Hana's heart gave a little flop which owed nothing either to nerves or anger, but she took a deep breath and walked firmly, not quickly and certainly not slowly, along the path towards him, reaching his side just as he stretched up to wind a piece of wire about a nail close to the top of the wall.

'Mr Carlyon?' It gave her some satisfaction, made her feel she was in control of the situation when she saw that he was startled. When he turned Hana found herself at the receiving end of a very critical look from probing, rather deep-set eyes. Eyes which had a bewildering familiarity in a face she knew she had never seen before.

'Hasn't anyone ever told you that it's foolish to creep up behind people?' The intense gaze raked her, to her chagrin showing none of the interest she was only too used to seeing when she met a man for the first time.

'I didn't creep.' Now that she had begun she found some of her confidence reasserting itself. How dared this—this philanderer, criticise her? 'I walked along the path in a perfectly normal manner.'

'Oh?' His initial irritation seemed to evaporate and he raised one dark eyebrow, at the same time easing himself back on the top step of the ladder while he continued to appraise her, now with a slightly warmer manner, at last reaching her feet where his eyes lingered on her soft soled shoes. 'You could have fooled me.' With irritating casualness he reached into the breast pocket of his shirt and took out a pipe which he proceeded to light, puffing while he looked at her with a slightly narrowed but still very percipient gaze.

Hana waited for him to say something, to ask what she wanted, but he showed no sign of doing so and, feeling a faint warmth in her cheeks, she repeated her first query, this time in even cooler tones than she had used at first. 'Are you Mr Carlyon?'

He inclined his head gravely, still without speaking, still watching her with that curiously familiar perception, mixed with just a touch of amusement.

'Mr John Carlyon?' Her chin went up while the disdain in her manner increased.

'That's me.' He took the pipe from his mouth, put it on the top of the wall, then, before she knew what he was about, he had sprung down from his perch to stand on the path immediately in front of her.

Some instinct of self-preservation made her take a step back. He was so large. And for such a large man so quick and light on his feet. Something of her feelings must have made themselves obvious for she could see quite blatant signs of laughter now.

'He's tall, dark and handsome.' Kim Barclay's tearful description came back to her as she stared up at him. She wouldn't have thought that she and Kim *could* have the same taste in men, but . . . It was impossible to disagree with it, cliché though it was. He was just the kind of man who could sweep a girl off her feet. But one thing she couldn't forgive him. He, unlike the callow youth she had imagined, wasn't nineteen. String cut into her finger again and she held out the parcel.

'These are your things.' It was thrust into his hands.

'My things?' He sounded surprised, but doubtless he had had plenty of practice in this situation.

'Your things,' she repeated with a firm determination to leave him in no doubt about her opinion. 'The things you left in Kim's flat the last time you stayed with her.' The expression on his face made her frown. 'Kim Barclay. Don't tell me you've forgotten?' Suddenly all the pain of her experience with Lindsay returned to torment her, making her sound very scornful indeed and, she realised, a shade strident. 'And I might as well tell you,' brown eyes gleamed at him in anger, 'that she has no intention of seeing you again.'

'Hasn't she?' The irritation he had shown a moment earlier darkened his expression again. 'And might I ask,' his voice was slow and drawling now, 'just what it has to do with you. Where exactly do you fit in?'

'I'm a friend of Kim.' It wasn't quite true but this wasn't the time for absolute truth. 'And I don't like seeing her hurt.'

'Hurt?' The raised eyebrow was challenging.

'Yes, hurt.' But not like me, she cried silently. No-one has ever been hurt like me. 'She's just nineteen and quite frankly I find it rather disgusting that a man of your age should behave so badly. You're quite old enough to know better.' Her cheeks were flaming as she threw that at him.

'And you're quite old enough to know,' he took his time while he stared at her, his lips a straight line, his eyes dark flashing steel, 'that you'll get no thanks from Kim or . . . from anyone for acting like an interfering busybody.' His manner was deliberately insulting.

'I've no intention of standing here all afternoon arguing with you.' Hana realised that if she didn't make her escape soon she was in danger of disgracing herself, worse, of making herself ridiculous by bursting into tears. 'I've done what I was asked to do.' Although this wasn't quite true it certainly wasn't the time to admit to being a volunteer. 'No more, no less.'

'Thank you.' His sardonic tone made her colour up even more, but before he could say more she whirled away from him, making a conscious effort to stop herself running along the path towards the door in the wall. When she reached it, she knew without looking back that he was standing where she had left him and that he was watching her with that speculative expression which she had found so disconcerting throughout the few minutes she had been with him.

It was a relief to be back in her car, to be able to reverse into a gate and accelerate down the hill, through the village and to reach the main road before she could begin to sort out her jumbled emotions. And then, as she drove along in the direction of her final destination, she caught sight of a picnic area and drew into it with a sigh of relief.

A moment later she had her shaking hands linked round a cup of coffee which she had poured from a flask. I handled it badly, she thought. With all the experience I have had about keeping cool in difficult situations I allowed my emotions to run away with me. She sipped the scalding coffee, blaming that for bringing the sting of tears to her eyes. But deep down she knew that they were the result of something more basic—part home-sickness, part anxiety about the new job she had to take over next week, but mainly sheer misery that all the plans she had made over the last years had come to such an ignominious end.

*   *   *

It had been love at first sight with Lindsay and herself when he had first appeared in the great London Hospital where Hana had just completed her training as a State Registered Nurse. In fact, she had been wearing the sought-after purple and white striped uniform for the very first time, ridiculously proud of the tiny cap, all intricate tucks, perched on top of her blonde head when he, going along the corridor with a group of senior doctors had given her a decidedly come hither look. They had been introduced the very next night at a party being thrown by Jane Evans to celebrate her engagement to Hamish Coverdale and Lindsay had quickly made it clear to everyone else that he regarded Hana as his very special property.

'I've been scouring the hospital all day for you,' he told her quite seriously as he manoeuvred her into a corner at the party. 'In the end I was beginning to wonder if you were a figment of my imagination.'

Hana knew enough about medical students and young doctors to take what he said with a pinch of salt. 'Really?' Although her voice was cool her eyes were laughing at him. 'You could have fooled me. Considering that we met at the very door of Grace Ward you didn't show a great deal of persistence.'

'Ah, Grace Ward.' With one palm he struck his forehead. 'That was the next on my list. But, at least, now I know that you noticed me. Even though I was the least significant of the clutch of doctors who passed you.'

'Oh, one always notices new faces. Even in a place like the London.' Not for worlds would Hana have confirmed what she was certain he knew well enough already, that he had the kind of looks that any girl would notice. 'And besides, I was feeling particularly pleased with myself. It was the first time I had on my SRN's uniform.'

'Ah, I see.' The intensely blue eyes had danced. 'Can you explain why it is that if you put an attractive girl into a uniform that's the wrong length, out of date, one that hides every natural curve of her body, and stick a ridiculous cap on the top of her head, she ends up looking twice as fetching as she ought to be? Can you explain that to me?'

'If I had known it had that dramatic effect I would have worn it tonight.' Not for anything would she have let him know how piqued she felt that he wasn't more impressed with the dress she was wearing.

'Oh, I'm not complaining.' His eyes had moved with lazy appreciation over the clinging blue jersey, over the bare shoulders and the narrow halter strap. 'I thought I had made that clear enough. I'm just asking about that other point.'

'That I can't explain. But then, I'm not a man.'

'Go on. You all know you look irresistible.'

'All of us?' she pouted provokingly.

'Well perhaps not *all*. Let's exclude Sister Chalmers and one or two others.'

'Maybe it's something to do with our work.' She adopted a soulful expression. 'The cool hand on the forehead, the soothing presence in the dark hours of the night.'

'Maybe.' He appeared to consider. 'On the other hand, there's the enema just after breakfast and the lanced boil just before lunch.'

'Oh, and I thought you were a romantic!' Laughing, Hana had made her escape in response to an appealing look from Jane and had taken a perverse pleasure in avoiding him for the rest of the evening.

But that hadn't prevented Lindsay from seeing Hana back to the Nurses' Home where she had had a room at that time. In company with some of the other nurses of course, but from then on it had been surprising how often he seemed to have business that brought him along to Grace Ward when he knew Hana would be on duty. And soon she had given up all pretence that she wanted to avoid him. It would have been pointless and impossible to do considering the speed with which she fell rapidly, inextricably, in love with him.

It had been his light-hearted approach to life as much as his looks and charm that had made him so irresistible to Hana, such a contrast, she decided, to so many of the young doctors who took themselves too seriously, some of them in fact were downright pompous. But to Lindsay life was one long joke, something to be enjoyed in the most positive way possible. Even looming exams could do nothing to dampen his irrepressible personality.

There were times, just occasionally, when Hana wished he would restrain his buoyancy, only a little, but no effort on her part had the slightest effect and, anyway, deep-down she preferred him as he was. And she knew they were ideally matched, complementing each other so her role developed into one of restraint and encouragement. In fact, she had to face the certainty that if it hadn't been for her patience, the hours she sat by him, coaching, asking questions, prompting answers, then he might very well have failed his final exams. As it was he scraped through and then put on a spurt in time to secure a post of junior houseman at the hospital.

Even to herself Hana had been reluctant to admit that this success might have had something to do with her friendship with Janet Leishman whose husband was one of the senior physicians. Janet was Sister in Grace Ward, the girls having been friendly since Hana had first come to London and when Janet had married Toby Leishman in a quiet wedding Hana had been asked along as witness. Over the years the friendship had developed and when Janet had left to have her first baby Hana, at a very early age, had stepped into the vacant position. It seemed a betrayal of Lindsay to think that his wildly celebrated appointment had anything to do with the friendship, but Toby was on the Committee and that might have been enough to clinch the decision. Whatever the reason, she was terribly grateful, to Fate, or Toby. Or maybe even both.

For the next year and a half Hana threw herself into what was now beginning to look like her life's work, that of tutoring Lindsay for some further qualifications which would enhance his chances in the future and which could possibly bring their wedding date just a bit closer. But when he failed them she felt that that day was as far away as it ever had been. She had blushed when Toby had teased her about it on one of the evenings when she went round to baby-sit for them.

'Why don't you take the exams yourself, Hana?' He walked into the children's room, tying his black tie, 'I think you'll know as much about it as Lindsay does.'

'Let me do that for you.' Before Hana could think of a reply his wife turned to him with a spark of impatience. 'And you'd better hurry or we'll be late.' Quickly she pushed him back through the door and turned to Hana with an apologetic look. 'Don't mind him, Hana. You know I've always said he was the world's most tactless man.'

Conscious that her smile was a trifle strained Hana brushed aside Janet's apology. 'I suppose I'll just have to get used to the idea that Lindsay isn't the kind who passes exams easily. He *does* try, but you know what he's like . . . And I don't really want him to be any different,' she finished loyally.

'Of course you don't,' Janet was determined to make things easier for her friend. 'And Toby thinks a lot of

Lindsay, he's always saying what a good doctor he is.'

'Thanks, Jan.' Hana's smile was a shade rueful. 'I know he's good with the patients. Unfortunately at the moment it's the piece of paper that's important. But never mind, he'll try again and he's sure to pass. At least,' she laughed, 'if I have anything to do with it he will. I'll work him day and night to make sure that he does.'

But in spite of her brave words Lindsay failed his exams next time and after his initial disappointment he had shrugged his shoulders and decided that it might be best to try to get a job overseas.

'After all,' his smile was a bit shame-faced, 'there are lots of jobs being advertised in the quality papers. In fact,' remembering, his voice became more enthusiastic and he threw off his dejection with the ease that was all too familiar to Hana, 'in fact, love, there was one for a couple in Abu Dhabi. Just last week it was. I wonder if I can lay my hands on the paper. They were looking for an MO for a private clinic.' He wrinkled his forehead as he tried to recall what he had read. 'And they suggested that there might be a job for a wife as well. Matron, it said. And they were offering a fabulous salary.'

'Oh Lindsay, I don't know. I like working here, you know that.'

'Yes, love I know.' Getting up from the sofa in Hana's small living-room, he linked his hands about her waist, pulling her close to him while he smiled down at her in the way he knew was most effective. 'But,' with his chin he forced her head back so that it was impossible for her to avoid his eyes, 'there's no sense in closing our minds to the opportunities that are available. Don't tell me that you wouldn't be equally happy—happier, dare I suggest—out there in some tropical paradise. And with me,

Hana,' he grinned in a way that disarmed any suspicion of conceit, 'how can you resist?' His smile had faded as he bent his head, brushing her lips in a way that made her pulses quicken. 'You know the way we're going on is hell on my nerves, darling.' He groaned and pulled her down onto the sofa beside him. 'It seems to me it's our only chance of getting married.'

'I don't know.' Hana tried to retain some control of her own emotions and, knowing that she was bound to fail, extricated herself from Lindsay's grasp and stood up abruptly. 'I really don't know why we can't be married and go on as we are. With both of our salaries we could be fairly comfortable, we might even save enough for the deposit on a house of our own.' They had been through the same argument so often that she had little hope of succeeding and wasn't surprised when Lindsay frowned and shook his head.

'I've told you before that I'm not going to get married, take on all the responsibilities, unless I have some decent prospects.'

'*You* take on all the responsibilities!' For once Hana allowed her own irritation full rein. 'I thought that was what marriage was about. *Sharing* the responsibilities. Everything wouldn't fall on your shoulders.' Angrily she walked away from him, into the kitchen where she filled the kettle and stood gazing out of the window without seeing anything.

'Sorry, Hana.' It wasn't long before she felt his arm round her waist, pulling her back against him, the rough rasp of his beard as he rubbed his cheek against hers. 'You know I didn't mean that.'

'No, that's the trouble.' She wasn't ready to forgive him, to say that it was all right—all the waiting for exam results, the disappointment, the strain of it was as wearing for her nerves as for his. 'That's what you always say.' Determinedly she moved away to switch off the kettle, reaching for some mugs and the jar of instant coffee. 'Sometimes I think, Lindsay, that you don't want any responsibilities, not in your work, not in your life.' The words and even more the tone of her voice seemed to crystallise the years of disappointment and she held her breath, waiting for the explosion she thought might come.

'That's below the belt, Hana. But I suppose I deserve it.' He seemed less upset than she had thought he might be. 'I suppose you're getting fed-up waiting and I don't blame you.'

It was so unlike Lindsay to be humbly contrite that in surprise she turned round to look at him, an expression of suspicion lurking in the eyes that scrutinised his features.

'Yes,' he went on, biting his lip in vexation while he seemed determined to avoid her searching gaze, 'but don't forget, love, just whose decision that has been. There hasn't been any need to wait. Not these days.' Suddenly the intensely blue eyes flicked up to look at her with that half-pleading, half-teasing expression which always had the ability to make her heart flip over. A surge of optimism began to stir in the base of her stomach in the instant before the drift of his words finally penetrated.

'Oh Lindsay . . .' She began to soften before re-membering they had been here before many times. 'What had you in mind?' Swiftly, before he had the opportunity to see the brilliance of her eyes, she turned back to the cups and began to spoon coffee into the mugs.

'You know, darling! Why can't we be up-to-date and try things out first. I don't see what harm it would do. If it worked out, and I have no doubts at all about that, then who knows, we could be running along to the registrar's before six months were up.'

'Mmm.' Hana gave the impression that she was considering what he had said. 'And what if it didn't?' Sombrely she handed him the cup and clutching her own led the way back to the sitting-room.

'Well, if it didn't,' carefully he watched her above the rim of the cup, 'if it didn't, darling, though I'm pretty sure that it would, then there's nothing lost, is there?' He shrugged boyishly and, watching him, Hana knew that when he reached the age of sixty he would still have about him that boyish, *immature* look.

'You really think that, don't you, Lindsay?' Hana lay back in her chair, trying to look as if none of this conversation was tearing her to pieces. 'You really think that if we lived together for a few months and then we decided that things hadn't worked out it would be simple just to finish. What if only one of us wanted to finish it, though, how would that affect things?' Her eyes narrowed as she stared at him.

'That wouldn't happen.' He tried to laugh the whole thing off. 'Things don't work out like that. And in any case, it wouldn't be any different if we were married, in fact it would be worse if we decided we had made a mistake.'

'No.' Bleakly she looked at him as if she were seeing him for the first time. 'That's what makes marriage different, Lindsay. You can't just walk out at the first sign of trouble, whereas if you're just living together . . .' She shrugged, hoping that he couldn't see how miserable she was. Clearly he didn't.

'But look at the fun we'd have, darling.' For some reason that she couldn't understand he seemed to sense that she was weakening, coming over to sit on the arm of her chair, taking the cup from her hand and putting it on the table, then pulling her head back against him, his fingers stroking her neck in a way he knew was effective. Hana was content to lie there toying with the idea for a while. After all, where was the harm in it? All the time it was happening and not even the hospital authorities bothered trying to stop it nowadays. It would be so easy. And, as Lindsay said, they would have such fun. Living with Lindsay would be *fun* there was no doubt about it.

But . . . Gradually the doubts, all the ones she had expressed before, slipped back into her mind, dismissing the easy solutions, reminding her that she couldn't bear to be the subject of the sidelong glances from the younger nurses, the pangs of jealousy she would be bound to experience when she saw Lindsay's easy flirtatious manner with them. And always, at the back of her mind, the knowledge that at any time he might decide that the fun had gone and walk out. And knowing Lindsay as she did, knowing his dislike of facing anything the least bit awkward, she would be a fool to pretend that his nature was anything other than weak and easy-going. That was one of the reasons she loved him so much. There was just a shade of protectiveness in her feelings for him. Making up her mind she put an apologetic hand on his, stilling the sensitive fingers.

'It wouldn't work, Lindsay. You must know that as well as I do.'

He had sighed dramatically then, coming round and pulling her to her feet as if he might force her by sheer brute strength. Then he had shrugged, accepting her decision with less than flattering philosophy. 'Well, it was worth a try, love. No hard feelings?'

'No hard feelings.' But although she had smiled she had felt despair.

'Trust me,' he had said when he left her that night. 'I'm determined to work some miracle whereby I'll be in the position to keep you in the manner to which you're accustomed.'

Entering into the spirit of the thing she had waved a hand round the not very exciting living-room of her furnished flat. 'Oh Doctor, you say the wildest things.'

'It's for you I care you know, Hana.' He wasn't at his most convincing just then. 'I hate not having the best to offer you.'

'These things don't matter.' For a moment she allowed herself to be persuaded by his protestations.

'I don't want you to be second best to Janet Leishman.'

'I wouldn't be, don't you see that Lindsay? With you I wouldn't be second best to anyone.' The words echoed round the room like a plea.

'Well, I'll have to see what I can do.'

And shortly afterwards he had gone and Hana was alone in the flat, wondering with a vague sense of unreality why it was that a man who looked like a Greek God could have this curiously unromantic streak. Take away all the non-stop patter for the nurses who flocked round him and he really was just a bit mundane. She had seen Toby who had been married to Janet for umpteen years being twice as romantic as Lindsay ever was even when they were alone together. Not that she minded, but she did sometimes wonder . . . she got the impression that all the impatience was on one side and she longed for him to sweep her off in a wild burst of impetuosity. If he had ever indicated that he couldn't wait for her any longer then she might have weakened and hang the consequences, but he hadn't and so she had never had the opportunity to make the grand gesture.

She ought to consider herself lucky that she wasn't subjected to all the stresses and persuasions that she had heard her contemporaries discuss. But somehow,

although she told herself *that* often enough she still felt
that in some subtle way she was missing out.

After the disappointment of Lindsay's failed exam,
life settled down into its normal routine and a sudden
rush in Grace Ward caused by an extra surgeon being
drafted in to help with the backlog of hip replacements
kept Hana from dwelling too much on her personal
disappointment. At least she was glad that there was no
studying to be considered at the moment, she didn't feel
fit to cope with that at the end of the day when she got
back from the ward. And she was so tired, even the fact
that she had seen little of Lindsay didn't properly register with her. Not until one Sunday when she had been
invited to Sunday lunch with Janet and Toby.

They were sitting in the large back garden of the house
in Wimbledon after lunch, drinking coffee and lazily
watching Justin and Crispin kicking a ball back and
forward to each other when Janet, with just the right
amount of casual unconcern in her voice, mentioned his
name.

'I'm sorry Lindsay couldn't come with you, Hana.'

'Yes.' Something indefinable in her friend's manner
made Hana hesitate before she answered fully. 'He
seems to have been as busy the last few weeks as I've
been. And unfortunately, always at different times. And
this weekend he had promised to go home and see his
mother. If I had been off yesterday we could have gone
together, but as it is . . .' She shrugged and then sighed
without realising she was doing so.

'Do you know Hester Brownlow, Hana?' Toby was
lying back with his eyes closed, ignorant of the intense
warning look his wife gave him. But Hana saw it and
raised her eyebrows in enquiry as she answered.

'Slightly. I usually speak to Miss Grenville when I go
along to Physio, but Hester was in the ward last week.

She's dealing with one of the patients in Grace.' She paused, waiting for some explanation for the original query, then when none came, 'Why do you ask, Toby?'

'What?' He started, jerking himself awake, then closing his eyes comfortably. 'Why do I ask what?'

Hana's amused glance in Janet's direction was ignored but she thought that she intercepted a warning touch from the wife to the husband.

'Oh, it doesn't matter.' For no reason that she could explain Hana felt disturbed but followed willingly when Janet got up and they joined the children in their game of football.

But the strange little incident was explained just a day or two later when she was emerging from the main door of the hospital and stood for a few moments, breathing in the cool fresh air at the top of the steps above the car park. Then she saw the familiar yellow sports car and Lindsay, keys in his hand, just unlocking the door. She was about to run down the flight of steps when she realised that he was speaking to someone, someone small and dark who had apparently said something very amusing for he was laughing as he held the door open while she made herself comfortable inside.

Without thinking what she was doing Hana walked down the steps towards the car, her heart beating in an uncomfortable, almost painful way. She heard the engine being switched on and had just reached the rear bumper when Lindsay's voice, clear as ever, easy and charming, drifted towards her through the open window.

'Did you say that your father would be at home, Hester?'

There was a murmur which the listener could not hear above the roar of the engine but which could only have been an affirmative reply for Lindsay's words reached her loud and clear.

'Then this is it, love, best foot forward and all that.' And they were off in a puff of exhaust smoke.

Afterwards Hana was rather pleased that her progress from the hospital didn't even falter. No-one watching from even the gallery positions of the upstairs windows would have known what a shock she had just had. Oh, they might have seen Lindsay getting into his car with someone other than the girl he had for the last five years been expected to marry, but that in itself wasn't totally inexplicable, there were all kinds of reasons why doctors and physiotherapists should drive off together, but . . .

Quickly Hana walked along the streets in the direction of her flat, trying to ignore the stabbing pain in the middle of her chest but giving way in relief when she closed her own front door behind her.

Lindsay. She rushed into her bedroom and threw herself onto the bed, clutching the pillow to her before submitting to the tears that had been welling up inside her. And when she began it was a long time before she was able to stop. It was as if she were expressing something which had been troubling her for a very long time, something which had been triggered into recognition by that tiny incident in the car park.

But at last the paroxysm passed and she was able to get up and go into the kitchen and make herself some tea. She stood looking out of the window, while all kinds of clues seemed suddenly to be resolved.

'Sorry, love, I can't,' Lindsay had told her apologetically when she had suggested that he come round to the flat as usual on Wednesday night. And he had wrinkled his nose, shuffled the pile of case notes in his hand while he tried to give the impression that he was hectically busy. 'Old Purves is having some kind of series of lectures.'

'Mr Purves!' At the time, even while she had noticed his slightly increased colour Hana had been surprised, for the senior surgeon was well-known for being so preoccupied with his private practice that he had little time to spare for extra duties at the hospital. But even then suspicion had been far from her mind.

'Yes, I'll explain some time. Now I must fly.' And with that he was disappearing along the corridor at a great rate, the tails of his white coat blowing behind him.

There had been one or two such incidents, each of them annoying at the time but now that she put them together they began to assume a wholly different perspective. And then, she remembered like a blow, there were Toby's casual words the other weekend. So, everyone must know about it. Her skin crawled with the humiliation of it. Everyone at the hospital must know. Everyone except herself she decided dramatically and the tears stung her eyes again.

But then a different, a more optimistic aspect of the situation occurred to her, something which brought hope surging back into her heart with renewed strength. It was something Lindsay was planning as a complete surprise to her. Of course. As soon as the idea occurred to her the ache in her chest melted, all her fears vanished. Of course, that was it! And the vague uneasiness she had felt was simply because somewhere at the back of her mind she had registered that Hester Brownlow's father run a fashionable clinic in Harley Street.

He must be thinking of trying for a job there. That was the marvellous explanation that raced through her mind. He had been curiously silent about his original plan of getting a job overseas and that was why. He must have heard of a vacancy in the clinic and he was hoping to get it and present her with the news as a gift. Relief suffused her like a warm bath. And if Lindsay was prepared to cultivate the daughter to get the job, so what?

Two days later the announcement of the engagement was in *The Times*. She didn't see it on the actual day although she had intercepted one or two curious glances in the ward as well as experiencing a reticent sympathy in the Sisters' Rest Room.

'You all right, Dean?' Sister Laycock who was senior midwifery tutor put a concerned hand on Hana's shoulder as she passed by while she was drinking her coffee.

'Yes, I'm fine.' Her smile had been as genuine as she could make it, for all her doubts, all her anxieties, had returned since the evaporation of the first euphoria. 'Thanks, Sister.' And she had returned to her *Nursing Journal*.

It wasn't until that evening that she learned the news and she was grateful that it was from Janet she heard it. Janet who had parked the children on her neighbour and had driven in to pick up Hana when she came off duty.

'Hello,' Hana smiled in surprise when she saw the familiar station waggon pulled up at the front steps. 'Waiting for your lord and master.'

'No.' Janet seemed reluctant to look directly at her friend. 'I came to see you actually. Toby won't be finished till seven so I'll run you back to the flat first.'

'This is luxury.' She settled back in the comfortable seats and waited till they had driven out onto the road. 'How are the boys?'

'They're fine. Probably driving Mrs Holford quietly round the bend. I only hope she's done what I said and put all her precious bits of Meissen away.'

Hana laughed, only slightly surprised at the concentration her friend was applying to her driving. 'I'm sure she will, so don't worry. It must have been something pretty important to bring you all this way through the rush hour traffic. To see me, you said?'

'Just a minute, love.' Carefully Janet negotiated her way between a wobbling cyclist and a heavy lorry winking to turn right. 'These people on bikes don't know the risks they're taking.' And then, as she seemed disinclined for further conversation, nothing more was said.

But when they reached the flat, Janet, with an air of determination, pulled a paper from her handbag. 'I gather you haven't seen this, Hana.' She pushed the folded page towards Hana and, turning away, busied herself with the kettle.

For a moment Hana's eyes refused to focus, the words swam about on the page until at last the ones that were relevant sprang out at her.

The moan that came from her lips was painful to hear and she didn't notice that her friend led her to a chair and forced her down onto it. Her hand went to her mouth and she bit fiercely into her forefinger, not feeling the pain.

'But he can't be.' It was a long time before she raised her eyes to look at Janet, unconscious that her eyes were dark with anguish, that her lips trembled as she spoke. 'It says here, Jan, that . . .' Again her eyes sought the printed page. 'It says here that Lindsay is going to marry Hester Brownlow. There must be some mistake.'

'I wish there were, love.' Janet put down a mug of tea and pushed it across the table before sitting down with her own. 'Do you mean to say, Hana, that you knew nothing about it?'

'No.' Feverishly she bit her lips. 'No I didn't.' In spite of her efforts a sob escaped but she appeared not to notice. 'I saw them together the other day. I couldn't think . . .' She shook her head as if in some way that would make the matter clearer to her. 'I couldn't think

why. And then . . .' Suddenly it seemed too pathetic to
tell her friend how in the end she had justified it to
herself and besides she couldn't speak for the tears that
were streaming down her cheeks.

The rest of the evening remained a blur to her. She
was aware of Janet trying to persuade her to go back to
Wimbledon, to stay there until she had got over the
shock. She remembered Toby coming to the flat, grim-
faced but kind, pouring her a glass of whisky and standing over her while she took it, then adding his persuasions to Janet's.

But Hana, who had never been intransigent, refused
point blank to leave her flat. She had no idea what she
meant to do but she had no inclination to run away from
whatever had to be faced. In the end she convinced them
that she would rather be left, refusing even Janet's offer
to stay the night with her, looking forward with desperation to the time when the door would close behind them.

And when at last it did, she lay in the dark, unable to
weep.

No-one, not even Janet, knew what it cost her to go
through the following weeks. She even managed to
congratulate Lindsay and Hester when she met them in
the corridor one day, smiling and holding her eyes wide
so that anyone watching them might have been forgiven
for thinking that she had never been in love with him
after all. Lindsay was the one who had been unable to
hide his feelings of embarrassment, so that Hana
thought people might imagine *she* had thrown *him* over
and that Hester Brownlow caught him on the rebound.

But the act could stretch only so far and when she saw
an advertisement for a sister's position in a small cottage
hospital in Bridgestead she sent in her application and
prayed. And when she received the letter confirming

her appointment she was only too pleased to be able to leave the hospital where she had worked for so long and which she had loved.

It was during her last week in London that Kim Barclay's problems were thrust upon her. And it was just an unlucky chance that it happened when her nerves were ragged with the emotional distress caused by saying goodbye to all the colleagues who had been good friends for so long, when she was exhausted by the brave front she was keeping up in an effort to convince everyone that her heart was undamaged.

That was what caused her to over-react when the sorry but not uncommon tale tumbled from the girl's trembling lips.

'You see, he said he would write to me, Sister. But it's been two months and I haven't heard.'

'You're sure you're not pregnant, Nurse?'

'Oh no, I'm not, Sister. It's not that, only . . . I did hope we would get married.'

'Did he ask you to marry him?' Hana's lips were a tight gash in her face.

'Not exactly,' Nurse Barclay sobbed. 'Only I thought that's what he meant. When he took me down, showed me his house and . . .' She hesitated and blushed.

'Took you to his house?' Hana felt her anger at this unknown man boil up within her. Men, were they all unreliable, irresponsible, interested solely in their own gratification? 'Where was this, Kim?' At that moment she was prepared to rush round and face him with the results of his brief affair.

'Oh,' under the influence of Sister's more personal manner Kim Barclay dried her eyes. 'It was ever such a long way, Sister. Not near here at all. He has a lovely house down in Devon. Near a place called Bridgestead.'

'Bridgestead?' That took Hana by surprise.

'Yes. But the last time I saw him was in my flat. Kate, Nurse Jones, was away on leave and John stayed there. He's left a lot of his things in my wardrobe.'

'I think the best thing you can do is forget him, Nurse. And I hope you've learned a lesson and that next time you won't be so foolish.'

'Yes, Sister.'

'But as it happens I'm going down to Devon myself. I start my new job there next week, so if you like I can see that all this man's things are delivered to him. What did you say his name was?'

'John Carlyon, Sister.' The nurse had a dreamy note in her voice and jumped when she felt sister's icy glance.

'Right then.' Hana's voice was as grim as her expression. 'Bring those things to me before Friday and a note of the address. I'll see that he gets them back and then you can start with a clean sheet. But remember what I said, Nurse,' she ended, without any expectation that her advice would be followed.

'Yes, Sister. Thank you.'

And, Hana vowed silently as she applied herself to a few final tasks, this John Carlyon is going to hear exactly what I think of him. Only then, when she had got rid of this weight of bitterness inside her, only then would she herself be able to start with a clean sheet.

CHAPTER TWO

THE Cottage Hospital at Bridgestead was as different from the South London as it was possible to be. Built at the end of the nineteen twenties, it had been greatly enlarged in the fifties, but still it was tiny when compared with the great institutions of the capital. It was a pleasant sprawl of single-storey buildings set in attractive grounds, saved twice, so Hana was told, from the 'rationalisation' axe and now guaranteed till the end of the century.

'And even then I don't think the locals will allow it to go,' Mary Bishop who had been employed as a temporary sister for the last two months in Fleming Ward assured Hana. 'There's a fund to try to raise enough money to keep it going as a private hospital should it ever be threatened again. Ted's the treasurer.'

In the two days since she had started on her new job Hana had learned a great deal about Mary and her husband, although she hadn't yet met the lawyer who had a practice in Exeter. She had been told what she knew already, that Sister Elgin whose ward it had been had been tragically killed in a car accident and that the authorities had persuaded Mary to come back and take over until a new appointment was made.

'I was very glad that you could come so quickly,' Mary made no bones about her anxiety to return as soon as she could to domesticity and motherhood. 'Even though Ted's mother looks after Nicky for me, I don't find it easy to do two jobs. If it hadn't been that I was very attached to Fleming I wouldn't even have considered it. Besides, Ted doesn't like me working.'

The two girls had got on well from the first and any strangeness Hana felt in the new environment was quickly dispelled in the genuine efforts of the staff to make her feel at home. All except one—and Mary had dismissed Hana's doubts about the senior staff nurse.

'Don't worry about Frost. She's just disappointed that she didn't get your job.'

'Oh.' The news that the older woman had applied for the position was disconcerting. 'Well, she must resent me a bit.'

'Oh, she'll come round. In fact I had the same when I got the sister's job a year before I was married. She was senior to me then and thought she should have got it, and the same when poor Jean Elgin was appointed. She'll come round in the end.'

'Nevertheless . . . I wonder why she was turned down? It must make her feel humiliated.' Knowing quite a lot about that feeling herself she sympathised with the absent nurse.

'Oh, the governors think she's all right so long as she's fairly closely supervised, but she's inclined to break down if she has too much responsiblity. And this being a surgical ward, quite often there's a great deal of pressure. That's probably why you were regarded as being so suitable, Hana. I know that you were the unanimous choice of the board. Sister in a London Teaching Hospital. Makes one wonder exactly why you decided to leave. The opportunities must be much better there than they are here.'

'Oh, you know how it is.' With great diligence Hana applied herself to the study of some case histories. 'Time comes when you want a change and I had had enough of the city for a spell.'

'Do you have a family?'

'Yes. My father and mother live in Germany. Dad works for the army and I have a young sister. She's just seventeen. Eight years younger than me and spoiled rotten by everyone, myself included. Now,' she frowned over some of the tiny writing, glad to have the chance of changing the subject from personal matters, 'what about the amputation in bed five? Mr Ellis?'

'Oh, I think he'll be going out soon. Jake should be in at the end of the week and give him his discharge.'

'Jake?' Hana put down one folder and lifted up the next.

'The big white chief.' Mary grinned. 'He took off the foot after struggling for weeks to save it. But the limb had been so mangled in the accident. I told you it was caught in the belt of a machine in the local brickworks, didn't I?'

'Yes. And if you hadn't then I would have known anyway for the patient gives me a more horrific account of it each time he has the chance.'

'Well, he's only seventeen. I suppose being the central figure in a drama is important at that age.'

'Poor lad. I don't suppose he'll find it so dramatic when he leaves and has to learn to use a prosthesis.'

'No. But still, we've had terrific success teaching people to use artificial limbs. Physio is pretty well geared up here.'

'Yes, I'm sure.' Her dry tone made the other girl look at her for a moment in surprise, but Hana's calm face gave no clue about the unexpected twist of pain that the mere word had brought her. She had thought that she was getting over it, but she wasn't. Recovery was as far away as ever. Then the name that had been mentioned a few moments earlier popped back into the conversation, reminding her that her question hadn't been properly answered.

'Well of course Jake keeps them all on their toes. In physio just as much as in the wards.'

'Jake. Jake.' Hana sighed and tossed down the folder. 'It's a name I keep hearing. There were two juniors in the sluice yesterday having a real heart to heart and one of them became quite swoony so I got the impression that he must be something special. But I suppose there could be more than one.'

'There could be but I doubt if there is,' Mary said smugly. 'I don't think there can be more than one Jake Carlyon.'

'Jake . . . who?' Hana was still, sitting with her pen poised over a fresh white sheet of paper.

'Carlyon. He's a bit of a dish really.' Mary seemed not to notice the other girl's curiously pale face. 'If it wasn't for Ted, I might even fancy him myself. What am I saying,' she laughed at herself, 'who am I kidding? I fancy him, Ted or no Ted. In common with ninety-nine per cent of all the females in the hospital.'

'Oh.' Hana picked up the notes and appeared to concentrate with considerable intensity. 'Carlyon. It's an unusual name isn't it?' She scarcely dared to breathe while she waited for the reply.

'What?' Mary had risen and was searching through one of the large metal filing cabinets. 'Carlyon? Not really. Not in this part of the country.' Finding what she wanted she returned to the desk and sat down beside the newly appointed Sister. 'The most unusual thing about him is the man himself, not the name.'

'You're making me more and more curious.' The only way to try to deal with her feelings of anxiety was to treat the matter lightly. 'I can hardly wait to meet this wonder-man.'

'Well, don't be like the rest of the females round about him. Don't let him see that you've fallen madly in love with him.' Pausing in the midst of her advice, Mary glanced up, her eyes travelling assessingly over the other girl's features, 'You never know, if you play your cards right you might just be the one to bring him to his knees.'

'I'm definitely not interested.' Hana's quick response owed more to her damaged emotions than to consideration and caused her companion to look at her even more speculatively.

'Oh?' She hesitated. 'You're not engaged, or anything are you, Hana?'

'No. Nor anything.' In spite of her determination to hide her feelings the bitterness in her voice was not lost on the other girl. But Hana's anxiety and curiosity as to the identity of the man they had been discussing could not be entirely swept aside. 'I gather that there's no Mrs Carlyon, then?' The papers rustled in her hands.

'No. Not yet.' Mary laughed. 'I think up till now Jake has had no need to take on the responsibilities that go with marriage.' The words so innocently spoken had an effect she could scarcely have foreseen.

'Just the kind of man I despise.' Hana tried to convince herself how much better she was without the Lindsay Andersons, or the John Carlyons of this world.

'Oh, steady on.' Mary was startled by the other girl's tone. 'If women throw themselves at a man then you can hardly blame the man for that. It's the women who are the fools. But there,' she shrugged and grinned, 'you're listening to a smug, happily married woman. Anyway . . . I'm sure the girls who have thrown themselves at Jake won't have anything to complain about, so maybe there's something to be said for a free-wheeling attitude. If both sides enjoy it who's to say it's wrong?'

Her words echoed in Hana's head so that she hardly

heard what Mary said next. Instead she was wondering, for the hundredth time, if things would have been easier for her if she hadn't maintained her straight-faced attitude in face of Lindsay's persuasions. If she had had some *real* memories to sustain her instead of this sense of total loss would it have been . . . Numbly she looked up at her companion, aware that she was being asked a question.

'Sorry, Mary. What did you say?'

'I was saying that you must have met Jake yourself so you must know what he looks like.'

'Must have met . . . ?'

'At your interview.'

'Oh.' Relief flowing through her made her realise just how worried she had been by the prospect of having alienated one of the senior surgeons at the hospital. 'I didn't catch all the names.'

'Oh yes,' Mary was quite definite. 'He's always on the interviewing boards. No-one would dare appoint a sister in one of his wards without his say-so. Anyway,' a swift glance at her watch reminded Mary of the passage of time, 'another half-hour and all will be revealed. We'd better do a swift round of the ward before they come. Jake's not like some of the older doctors,' she reassured as they emerged from sister's office, 'he's not a great one for protocol. But woe betide anyone who gets things mixed.' Mary's pretty face was transformed by a grimace supposed to represent abject terror. 'Just don't let him catch you out, that's all.'

The next forty minutes passed in such a scurry of preparations for the consultants' rounds that Hana had little time to dwell on her own particular anxieties. She tried to deal diplomatically with Staff Nurse Frost, whose manner was as cool as her name, then became involved in showing a junior how best to cope with dressings for a patient who had recently had a colostomy. In fact the girl showed so much ineptitude that the man was becoming upset and Hana thought it was best to complete the job herself.

Then, just as she emerged from the curtained bedside, she noticed that her crisply starched apron had an unpleasant stain and she hurried off to the sluice room where fresh uniforms were kept. It was a few moments before she emerged, feeling more than a little dishevelled, tucking a strand of hair beneath her cap as she hurried across to the office.

The murmur of voices told her what she had been afraid of, that the doctors had arrived when she had been changing her apron, and feeling shy, embarrassed, just a little at a disadvantage, she pushed open the door and went into the room which was uncomfortably crowded with white-coated figures.

'Oh, here she is.' Mary's relief was transparently obvious. 'Sister Dean,' there was an encouraging expression in her eyes as if she understood only too well just what Hana was going through, 'may I introduce Mr Castlereagh.'

Hana smiled as she held out her hand to the small round man who she remembered having seen at the interview.

'And this is Dr Jordan, Dr Aziz . . .' Mary went on as the two young doctors stood up. 'And Mr Carlyon.'

Only then did Hana realise that a figure hidden from her view had been leaning against one of the filing cabinets behind the door and as she swung round to look at him she felt the colour drain from her cheeks.

Those dark eyes which on Saturday she had thought she had seen before. Deepset. Intense. Of course she hadn't seen them. Only a hundred others like them, with that same probing analytical expression, the reflection of an experienced inquiring medical mind. And right now they were as cold as ice.

Defiantly she raised her chin half an inch as she returned his stare with equal coldness.

'Sister.' His nod was brief, just verging on rudeness.

'Mr Carlyon.' The colour flamed back into her face and to her relief she was almost immediately involved in a clinical discussion about a patient whose condition was causing some anxiety and then she was leading the small group towards the bed.

'Could we have curtains, Staff Nurse?' But as she turned to speak Hana found that Staff Nurse Frost had been diverted and was hurrying across the ward towards another patient.

'Nurse Jenkins, curtains please.' Seeing what she thought was a sardonic glance from Mr Carylon, Hana spoke more sharply to the girl than she had meant and even then it was too late for he had pulled the curtains himself and although he appeared to be deep in a discussion with the other doctors, his eyes were firmly fixed on Hana's blazing cheeks.

'What do you think, Sister?' The sudden question made Hana jump and it was only after some stammering that she was able to pick up the gist of the discussion and make some positive nursing suggestions.

'Well, how did you get on, love?' When at last the office door closed behind them Mary looked at Hana sympathetically. 'You look as if you need a cup of tea.'

'You could say that.' Determined that the misery she was feeling would be shared by no-one, Hana tried to smile. 'I don't think I impressed anyone.'

'Oh don't worry. They'll all understand and make allowances. It can be quite an experience, the first days in a new job. But tell me, what did you think of Jake? You'd remember him, of course.'

'No.' Hana's voice was casual as she told the lie. 'Certainly he wasn't at the interview. Otherwise I would have remembered.' *He's not the kind of man you forget. The last was a private reflection as she recalled the broad shoulders under the white coat, the thick curling hair, the sudden smile for patients whom he approved.*

'Wasn't at the interview.' Mary was lost in uncertainty. 'But he's always . . .' Then impatiently, 'But of course, he must have been in the States when they did the interviewing. I had forgotten that. He was over presenting a paper to the American equivalent of the BMA. And of course they had to arrange a replacement at short notice. I can't think why I forgot.' She laughed suddenly. 'I couldn't imagine why you weren't knocked all of a heap like the rest of us. So . . .' her eyes gleamed mischievously as Hana's words came back to her '. . . You were quite taken with him, were you?'

'He looks very nice.' Busily Hana scribbled notes into her diary. 'And Mr Castlereagh too. Are there many young doctors who do their training here?' With quiet determination she tried to divert attention to a less awkward subject and was relieved when her efforts appeared to be successful.

But when the day's work was over and she drove slowly back along the quiet country lanes to her cottage on the outskirts of Bridgestead it was impossible for her to conceal her dismay from herself. The feelings she had experienced when she turned round in her office to face the last man in the world she wished to see, returned to her. Her heart hammered in hard agitated strokes, her fingers round the steering wheel became clammy, her mind detached, unable to grapple with the bitter knowledge that this particular problem was of her own making.

It was with a feeling of relief that she turned into the

slightly overgrown drive, parked the car and got out. Tonight, she decided, she would start to tackle the garden. She would go in, make herself a meal, feed the cat and then get into some old jeans and start on some weeding. Work was the only way to get over the present awkward situation. If she worked so hard that she was exhausted, she would fall into bed and sleep soundly. Then and only then would she be able to cope with her work at the hospital with some degree of competence. Otherwise she might just as well put up the shutters and go back to London with her tail between her legs. It didn't seem to matter to her that she was mixing her metaphors wildly. And returning to London was something she refused to contemplate. She had allowed one man to drive her away. If she were to allow another to drive her back then she would quite simply have no self-respect left.

By the end of the first month in Bridgestead Hana was almost able to convince herself that Jake Carlyon had forgotten. Once or twice she had wondered, only when she was having a flight of fancy, but she had wondered if he had even recognised her. Then she would relive their first introduction in her office, would see again the icy depths in his dark eyes and the cool nod that could scarcely be the normal way to greet a new colleague.

But they had reached some kind of mutual tolerance, a feeling that, on her side at least, mingled with respect. For he was a good surgeon. No amount of prejudice on her side could blind her to that and she was prepared to admit that many of the most eminent names in London were no better. He was popular with patients and staff alike, a fact that caused her a certain amount of pique in the early days, when Mary had gone and she was alone in charge of the ward. An old man who had come in for hip replacement surgery had quavered at her nervously when she spoke to him on the afternoon before his operation.

'It will be Mr Carlyon, Sister? Who does the operation I mean.'

'I'm not absolutely certain, Mr Goudge.' In London it had been the practice to avoid questions of this kind, although in Bridgestead it was more possible for patients to see only one surgeon throughout their treatment. 'I think there's a good chance.'

'I was told it would be Mr Carlyon,' the old man worried. 'I know he's the best.'

'All our surgeons are excellent, Mr Goudge. I don't think you need worry about the operation.'

'Oh but . . .'

At that moment there was a firm step on the floor and the curtains were parted so that Mr Carlyon could slide into the small cubicle. Without glancing at Hana he held out a hand for the notes which she passed over. She stood, victim of her usual reaction but trying to control the indignation, irritation and just plain antipathy that the man inevitably raised in her.

'I was just asking Sister, Doctor . . .' Relieved, Mr Goudge sank back on the pillow '. . . if you would be doing the operation yourself.'

'Of course.' His voice was calm and equable as it usually was. 'I told you that when I saw you last in Outpatients, didn't I?'

'Yes. Yes, you did. But when Sister didn't seem certain . . .'

'Sister?' For the first time he swung round in Hana's direction, one dark eyebrow raised interrogatively. 'Of course Sister knows I'm operating.' His expression changed to a reassuring smile as he returned to the patient. 'Now, I'm just going to have a last look at your hip. But why you should imagine that I'd allow anyone else to operate I just don't know.'

But when they returned to her office politeness at least on his side evaporated. 'I make it a practice, Sister,' coldly his eyes looked into hers, showing none of the admiration she was used to seeing—neither her looks nor her efficiency had any appeal for Jake Carlyon it seemed—'to try to reassure patients. Especially the elderly, especially the day before a major operation.'

'Of course.' Her calm manner belied the turmoil inside her. 'That is *basic* medical practice.' And she felt a tiny shiver of triumph when his eyes narrowed slightly.

He answered only after a pause, 'What I meant, Sister, is that I can't understand why you should worry Mr Goudge by telling him that I might not be doing his operation.'

'Did I tell him that?' Then, feeling that she might be on delicate ground, 'Sir?'

'That was the impression I got.'

'Oh, then I'm sorry you got it wrong.' She smiled sweetly. 'Mr Goudge asked me if I was certain you would do the operation and I told him that I thought there was a good chance.'

'Come, Sister, you must have known I would be in theatre tomorrow.'

'I was always told that I was not in the position to give an absolute assurance on these things. That I should be very certain indeed before I made any firm promise to a patient.'

'Highly commendable I'm sure, Sister.' The faint smile on Jake Carlyon's lips found no reflection in his eyes. 'But in future I would prefer it if you were to be more specific. After this, if anyone seeks such a reassurance then you have my permission to give it.' He put a hand on the door handle, pulling it towards him. 'I think

I can guarantee that if I have promised to operate on a patient, I shan't break that promise.'

'Very well, sir.' Hana smiled as she shuffled her papers. 'But I suppose that's a promise Sister Elgin might have made too.'

In the long pause that followed he glared at her while she tried to show an ease she was miles from feeling. 'Well, even my most devoted patients won't expect me to perform miracles, Sister. But don't try putting me in my grave just yet. I'm not in the mood to be so obliging.' And before she had time to reply, or even to think of something suitably cutting, the office door had closed, none too gently, behind him.

But such spats were few and far between. Perhaps because each of them was too conscious of the vulnerability of their work to allow personal feelings to disrupt the harmony of the ward. And perhaps because Hana was so busy trying to avert trouble with Staff Nurse Frost she had little time for crossing swords with Jake Carlyon.

But she was glad when an invitation from Mary reached her asking her to come along for a meal on Saturday night. Glad because it was the first she had received since her arrival in Bridgestead and she was growing bored with her own company. Glad because she had missed Mary when she had left the ward and looked forward to exchanging gossip with her again.

So when she began to get ready for her outing she found herself, for the first time in months, singing as she applied some make-up to her cheeks. It was such a surprising sound that she looked at her reflection in consternation before allowing a smile to curve the generous mouth. Then, in an excess of amused disbelief, she daringly touched her long, intensely dark lashes with some gold mascara which she had completely forgotten.

The song was still on her lips as she turned to give a

final check to her reflection. Short dress, Mary had said, and this one, ridiculously inexpensive as it had been, should fit the bill. It reached just below the knees and the full skirt swirled seductively when she moved. The neckline was deep and square, vibrant blues and greens of the fine cotton material providing a foil for her creamy, almost honey-coloured skin—after all that gardening—and the full elbow-length sleeves were just right for a dinner party. Round her neck she wore a short chain with a tiny piece of coral set in a deep blue cabuchon with matching drops in her ears.

You'll do, she assured herself smilingly as she reached for a large shawl to throw about her shoulders before she banged the door behind her and went out to the car.

'You must come up and see Nicky.' Mary was waiting for her at the door and when she had been introduced to Ted, Hana found herself being hurried upstairs. 'I've told him all about you and he won't go to sleep till he's seen you. This way . . . I say, Hana, you look quite different with your hair like that.'

'Hmm.' Hana shook her head, feeling the silky strands dance about her face. 'It wouldn't do like this in the wards. It would never be tidy. Besides being much too skittish for a serious ward sister.'

'Oh, don't get me wrong. You look fabulous with it on top, but this way makes you look years younger. And I like your dress. Nicky will be most impressed.' As she pushed open the bedroom door there was the sound of scuffling, muffled giggles and scarcely a twitch from the duvet which covered the bed completely.

It was some time before Nicky could be persuaded to emerge even partially from his hiding place and then it was more as a result of his mother's impatience than any apparent inclination of his own.

'Well, if you're not going to be sensible Hana and I will have to go downstairs. The other guests will be arriving soon and I can't stay here all night.'

'Maybe he would like me to read him a story.' When the covers were pushed down a few inches to reveal a pair of very mischievous dark eyes Hana stretched out a casual hand to pick up a book from a bedside table. 'I know two other little boys who love stories.'

'What are their names?'

'One is Justin and the other Crispin and they live in London.'

'I've been to London. Haven't I, Mummy.'

'Yes, you have, darling.' From downstairs the sound of the doorbell cut across the conversation and Mary bent swiftly and kissed her son. 'Now be a good boy and go to sleep. I must go downstairs.'

'But I want a story.'

'That's all right,' Hana's smile reassured Mary. 'Go and see to your guests, I'll read to Nicky. But,' she turned to the bed, 'it's got to be a short one.'

'All right.' Nicky grinned happily, turning round so that he could comfortably watch Hana while she sat in the circle of light from the bedside lamp.

Ten minutes later, she had just closed the bedroom door behind her when the doorbell went for the third time since her arrival and she was half-way downstairs when the voice that she knew so well, that for all its mellow quality she was beginning to dread, brought her progress to a sudden halt. And she was standing there, one hand on the banister, the evening light from a high window catching her hair, delicately illuminating the gauzy material of her dress, when he glanced up and paused in the midst of the conversation he was having with their host and hostess.

In that moment Hana knew that Jake Carlyon was

disconcerted. Just as disconcerted as she was. Neither of them had expected to see the other and he at least was not going to pretend that he found the surprise a pleasant one. Mary, apparently unconscious of the tension which had suddenly invaded her hall, was refreshingly casual.

'Bless you, love. Hana's been reading to Nicky.' She explained to the silent Jake Carlyon. 'But you two know each other so well that there's no need for introductions and that's why I didn't put you next to each other at dinner.' She grinned at Jake in a way that astonished Hana who had not known they were on such friendly terms. 'I don't see why you should always have the best-looking girls.'

As she descended the last few steps Hana sensed the great feeling of relief that Jake Carlyon was experiencing. And the knowledge that she shared his feeling did not prevent the wholly illogical resentment that immediately welled up inside her. How dared he be unwilling to sit beside her at dinner? Just because she had had the courage to tell him a few home truths. Truths which she supposed in his exalted position, he was unused to hearing.

She smiled sweetly at him as Mary and Ted spoke inconsequentially about nothing in particular, noticing in a detached way just how handsome he looked in the formal suit, how the pale cream silk of his shirt seemed to make him look more darkly forceful than ever. But when her expression was hidden from the Bishops she made sure that he could not mistake the message she was sending him, felt pleasure when the faint narrowing of his eyes admitted that he understood.

Count me out of your admiring harem, Mr Carlyon, she taunted. Even if the rest of my sex finds you irresistible, you don't appeal to me, not one little bit. You see,

I'm possibly the only one who knows what you're *really* like.

The smile she turned on Ted as he put his hand on her elbow to lead her into the sitting-room was almost dazzling and totally concealed the nagging pain which had just returned to the region of her heart.

CHAPTER THREE

IT WOULD have been so much easier if she had been sitting next to him, Hana thought contrarily as she smiled at something her neighbour on her right said. So much easier not to have to look straight across the table each time she raised her head, each time she put a morsel of food into her mouth. As she was placed, it was hard to avoid seeing what it was about him which made him so attractive to women.

There was something rather special in the way his eyes seemed to sparkle when he laughed, and it wasn't altogether the reflection of the flickering candles from the ends of the tables. And there was something nice about the way he treated the elderly woman on his left with the same teasing deferentiality he showed to the glamorous step-daughter on his other side. Hana tried to pay attention to what the girl's father was saying, it was a welcome diversion from the blatant fluttering of eyelashes which Jake Carlyon would find so appealing.

'I was asking, Hana,' James Catenby had told her in the first few minutes of their acquaintance that he always called pretty girls by their first names and insisted that they do likewise, 'I was asking just why you left London to come down here to the West Country to do your nursing.'

'Oh,' by this time Hana had the answer so pat that she had almost convinced herself, 'I simply felt the need of a change. I got tired of the city. I'm a country girl at heart, you know.' Conscious of a silence round the table she

found it impossible to control the faint colour in her
cheeks.

'And you're living out Lowculme way.' Trying to
remember what he had been told, James wrinkled his
brow, 'Is that right?'

'Yes. When I knew I had got the job I went to an estate
agent and found Rose Cottage had just come onto their
books so I went out to see Mrs Castle who owns it. She's
gone to Australia for six months to visit her son and
really wanted someone just to live in it. When I said I
liked cats and agreed to do the garden she fixed a very
low rent which I could easily afford.'

'And when Mrs Castle comes back?' There was a
speculative look on James Catenby's handsome face
when he looked at her. 'I hope that won't mean we'll be
in danger of losing you.'

'No, of course not.' Defiantly she looked across the
table as she spoke, telling Jake Carlyon in no uncertain
terms that there was no chance of getting rid of her.
Recollection of his jibes still stung just a little and she
was glad of the opportunity of assuring him of her
determination to stay. 'My original plan was to buy a
small cottage but the prices are so high! I did wonder if I
might persuade my parents to invest in a house for their
retirement, but I'm still hoping that I'll find something
that's within my means.'

'Perhaps James will be able to help you, Hana.' Mary
got up and began to collect plates. 'He has interests in
property and might know what's happening in the area.'

'Yes.' Ted rose to help his wife. 'There's not much
that James doesn't know about. He's the right man to
cultivate, Hana. Chairman of the local council, on every
committee going, including the hospital.'

'Oh.' Hana looked round at him, seeing what she had
noticed immediately they were introduced, the smooth

self-assurance of the man, the handsome silver-haired good looks which didn't quite equate with his wife's quiet dowdy exterior but which was apparent in his daughter's extrovert vivaciousness. And it was Tanya who spoke now.

'Yes, anything you want to know you should ask Daddy. I've never met anyone who can put you on to the right man as quickly as he can.' She put a hand on Jake's dark sleeve, spreading out her fingers so that the pink tinted almond-shaped fingernails showed to the best advantage, 'If you've any problems, he'll smooth them out in next to no time.'

'I'll remember that.' He smiled down at her, then raised his eyes suddenly to encounter Hana's disapproval.

'What I can't understand,' James Catenby brought the conversation back to where his curiosity could be satisfied, 'is why a girl like you should be on her own. Don't you find Rose Cottage just a bit quiet?'

'Not a bit.' Hana's voice was cool, discouraging. 'I like it. By the time I've finished the day's work it's what I need. Peaceful, not quiet. And there's enough work in the garden to fill any idle moments I might have.'

'Mmm,' he considered. 'I would have thought you might prefer it to have one of the other nurses living with you. It's all right in the summer but in the winter . . .'

'Oh that's one of the conditions of the lease, I've agreed to being the sole tenant. There's a lot of lovely old furniture and Mrs Castle didn't want anyone in the house who wouldn't look after it. And, as I say, it's what I want right now.' She was unaware of having made an admission in the last few words, but was pleased when the conversation veered off in a different direction and she was free to enjoy the delicious roast lamb which was the main course of the meal.

But by the time they had reached the pudding, a rich confection which consisted of piles of tiny choux buns filled with cream and decorated with spun sugar, Hana found that more and more her attention was wandering from what James on one side and Ted on the other were talking about, that she was straining to hear what was being said on the opposite side of the table, that she would have liked to enjoy some of the apparently endless strings of jokes with which Tanya Catenby amused Jake Carlyon.

It was only when there was a pause in the talk towards the end of the meal that she had the opportunity of hearing where the general conversation had led, when Mary, laughing at something Jake had been saying, brought in a name that had Hana's heart hammering against her chest in an excess of agitation.

'Oh, don't tease, Jake.' She lay back in her chair and wiped the tears from her eyes with a handkerchief. 'I just don't believe it. That sounds more like one of Jonathan's exploits than one of yours.'

'No.' He grinned at his hostess, shrugging slightly as if to admit that he didn't mean to be taken too seriously. 'I promise it happened just as I described.'

Hana sat staring, waiting for her agitation to die down, still uncertain what had caused it and then Mary got up, her amusement under control at last, and went to the sideboard to collect the cheeseboard which she placed in the centre of the table.

'I'll believe you, thousands wouldn't. Oh dear,' she sniffed. 'Excuse me. You shouldn't make me laugh so much. You wretch.' Playfully she tapped Jake reprovingly on the shoulder. Then, as she sat down, 'By the way, how is Jon these days? It seems ages since we heard anything about him.'

'As you say, "it seems ages".' Jake Carlyon seemed to

be staring at something just an inch above Hana's head. 'But then, you know Jon. He always was an inconsiderate young swine.'

Mary turned to Hana confidentially. 'We're talking about Jake's young cousin. His namesake in fact, isn't that right Jake?' Then, in response to his enquiring eyebrow, Mary went on, 'Jonathan *is* your namesake, isn't he?'

'I would want notice of that question.' Now Jake Carlyon seemed more than willing to allow his gaze to linger on Hana's face, to take note of her blazing cheeks, her eyes brilliant with embarrassment, then to allow the faintest smile of satisfaction to curl his lips. 'In fact,' at last his attention flicked towards his hostess, 'in fact, Mary, it might be more correct to say that we're both named after the same man, our grandfather. I just have the doubtful privilege of sharing a name with him.'

'Doubtful privilege,' Mary scoffed lightly. 'You know you don't mind a bit.'

'Most of the time I don't.' Again he allowed his attention to linger, with pointed blandness on Hana's features. 'But it can, just occasionally, lead to confusion.'

'Get away with you,' Mary surveyed him with a faintly maternal expression. 'No-one could really confuse you. Although there is a certain similarity. Same colouring, about the same height.'

'The lad hasn't been here for a long time. At least if he has I haven't seen him,' James Catenby said.

'Oh, he was here,' Tanya chimed in. 'I saw him about two months ago. When you were in the States I think, Jake.'

Hana allowed the rest of the evening to wash over her and afterwards could remember little of what was said after they rose from the table. Vaguely she heard Mrs

Catenby ask her if she would be interested in joining an embroidery class which was held in the church hall on Wednesday evenings. And she assumed that she had made some kind of excuse for the suggestion seemed to die a natural death.

Anyway, when the rest of the guests began to talk about going home she rose to her feet with an alacrity that made Mary look at her reproachfully. The Catenbys were just driving away, James at the wheel of his imposing limousine, when she came downstairs with the shawl she had left on the end of Nicky's bed.

'Thank you for a lovely evening. And the food was super, Mary.' It was an effort to appear wholly at ease and she was very conscious of the dark figure standing just inside the open door of the sitting-room. 'Goodnight, Mr Carlyon,' she called gaily. 'Goodnight, Ted.'

'Goodnight, Hana.' Smilingly he bent his head to kiss her. 'You know, I'll never trust my wife again. She told me you were good-looking but she didn't tell me you were a knock-out. Talk about feminine jealousy.' He squeezed his wife affectionately.

'Well, I know you're very susceptible.' His wife smiled up at him. 'Now you go and look after Jake and I'll see Hana off the premises.'

She shivered slightly as they stepped across to where Hana had parked her car, then spoke in a theatrically low voice. 'Why so formal with the boss? The whole idea of the evening was for you and Jake to get together.'

'You're wasting your time I'm afraid, Mary. But it was a lovely evening anyway. And perhaps it's best to keep to fairly distant relationships when we work so closely together.'

'Well, you must be the first nurse to think along those lines and anyway, Jake's not like that.'

'With me he is.' It was an effort to inject some

lightness into her voice. 'But . . . I didn't know you were on visiting terms with him. You didn't tell me.'

'Didn't I?' Mary sounded genuinely surprised. 'Well, I thought you knew.'

'It was a super evening, Mary. Thank you for asking me.' Now she was anxious to bring the evening to an end so she got into the car and slammed the door.

'Thanks for coming, love.' Mary waited while Hana switched on the engine but when she tried the starter, the motor gave a funny little whine and stopped. Twice, three times, she tried and each time with the same result. Panic made her turn the key time after time until the battery gave signs of fatigue and it was scarcely a surprise when the door was opened and Jake Carlyon thrust his head close to hers.

'All you're doing is wearing out the battery.' His tone was peremptory, edged with irritation, and the one least likely to appeal to her in her present mood.

'I'm aware of that,' she spoke without looking at him and her tone was cold. 'But I am rather anxious to get back home.'

'Well it's not going to start tonight.'

'In that case,' she pushed him aside, swinging her legs out of the car, 'I'd better get Mary to ring for a taxi.' It was impossible to hide her annoyance so she didn't begin to try. 'I'm sorry Ted. Will my car be in your way there?'

'Of course not. Besides it's Sunday tomorrow. And I know someone who'll come and have a look at it for you. Shall I give him a ring in the morning.'

'If you would I'd be grateful. And now, Mary, if I can trouble you to ring for a taxi.'

'A taxi,' Ted scoffed at the suggestion. 'And a man there just panting to run you home.'

'I wouldn't dream of taking Mr Carlyon out of his way.'

'Don't be daft, love. Besides, he can go round your way just as easily as any other. It'll put only half a mile onto his journey.'

'Oh but I couldn't, I . . .'

'Of course you'll come with me, Sister Dean.'

Hana found that a very firm hand was on her elbow and she was being propelled towards the red Jaguar which was such a familiar shape in the hospital car park. 'Now get in.' The words were hissed at her at the same time as the door was unlocked and she was thrust into the seat without feeling she had made any decision in the matter. Then, with a few more goodnights, they swept out of the drive and Hana was alone with the man she disliked more than anyone she had ever known.

The silence continued while they drove through the brightly lit streets of the small town, then, before she had time to do more than notice the few people who were still about, to watch the unsteady progress of one man as he tried to decide whether to cross with the lights or against them, they had left Bridgestead behind and were climbing out of the valley towards the hamlet of Low-culme.

'I'm sorry to put you to so much trouble.' The embarrassing silence forced the words from her lips.

'It's no trouble.'

On they drove, the headlights mesmerising in the way they rose and fell along the switchback road.

'I suppose you expect me to apologise to you.' She had had no intention of saying the words but the reaction they caused was so violent that she gasped and put a protective hand to her throat when he pulled savagely off the road and slammed on the car brakes.

'Do you think you should apologise?' In contrast to his action his voice was calm, indifferent almost. And as he waited for her to answer he slewed round in his seat, looking at her with such intensity that it was impossible for her to drag her eyes from his.

'N . . . n . . . no.' She hated herself for showing weakness in front of this man. This man who was so used to having everything his own way. Like most men. 'Of course I don't.' Her courage was returning, the excited hammering of her heart slowed to a less frightening pace. 'But if an apology would please you then I'll be happy to give you one.' She made up her mind that drawling condescension would irritate this man more than anything and had the reward of seeing his lips tighten.

Then, with an abrupt change of mood, they relaxed, curved into a smile. 'Let me assure you, Sister Dean . . .' his eyes wandered lazily over her face, moved to the low neckline of her dress where they lingered for a moment before coming back to her face, 'if I cared about it enough then I could soon extract . . . an apology from you.'

'Do you really think so?' Tension was mounting inside her again, bringing back the tremor to her voice. Physical awareness of him had struck even more forcibly in that moment of his veiled threat, when he reminded her that as a man he was not uncertain of his own powers. 'You flatter yourself.'

To her dismay he put back his head and laughed. Laughed in the way he had done earlier when they were having dinner, when Tanya had said something that amused him. The sound was such an unexpected pleasure that she felt a tingling in her senses, there was an inclination to join him in laughing, at what she had no idea, and at the same moment there was the contradictory sting of tears behind her eyes.

'Come on, Hana!' The deep mellow notes of his voice were even more attractive now when she slackened her grip on the resentment she felt for him. 'What are we quarrelling about? Don't you think it's pretty futile?' She saw his hand go out in the semi-darkness, a finger touched the switch and the headlights were extinguished.

All breath was expelled from her body in a shuddering sigh. The outline of his face was vague and shadowy in the sudden darkness and she longed to put out a hand to trace it with a teasing finger. As if he could read her thoughts she felt his touch on her cheek, a gentle trickle that had all her feelings, all her bruised emotions clamouring for some salve. Without realising what she was doing she leaned slightly against him, accepting the hand that slipped beneath her hair, stroking the nape of her neck once or twice, then pulling her insistently against him.

And his mouth offered the balm she craved. Although she hadn't understood that balm could take such a dizzying, distracting form. And when at last he relinquished her lips his mouth moved to her eyes, to her hair, where he seemed to find the lingering scents of the Chanel she had sprayed so freely before leaving home that evening.

Scarcely realising what she was doing Hana raised her hands, twining her fingers in his hair, feeling its smooth clean springiness while imperceptibly she guided him as his lips sought the hollow at the base of her throat. And then quite abruptly he was moving away from her, a white shape in the darkness was his hand going out to switch on the ignition. His eyes glittered at her with a fierce antagonism in the instant before the lights came on, illuminating his features with a relentless glow. When he spoke, it was with his usual self-assurance, in a way meant to tell her very forcibly that he had felt no involvement in that kiss.

'I accept your apology, Sister Dean.'

It was shock that made her hand reach out with lightning speed and strike him hard across the face. And pride would not allow her to show the instant regret, and even a ripple of fear, she felt as the dark eyes blazed unmistakably before their expression was quickly shaded.

'You brute,' she hissed between tightly clenched teeth.

'And I was about to tell you that I found you irresistible, Sister.'

'Please.' Perhaps it was the ache in her chest that brought the pleading note to her voice. Hearing it she thought that he must be aware of it, take some notice. 'Please,' she repeated, 'take me home.'

Although she looked away from him, she was aware of the smile that hovered about his lips, but even so was unprepared for the scorn that sounded in his voice as he drawled, 'Of course, that was the idea after all. But I find you intriguing, Sister.'

'Really?' Her voice was chipped ice.

'Yes. What is it, I ask myself, what is it gives a woman like you, reasonably attractive, reasonably intelligent, such an outsize chip on her shoulder. What did some man do to you?'

Reasonably attractive. *Reasonably* intelligent. Somehow the qualifications were the most wounding words he had spoken to her yet and her hurt showed in the passionate way she turned round to him. 'Why is it that men always think you've had your heart broken? Don't be so ridiculous! Can't you even begin to imagine that some women can live quite happily without a man in tow?'

'Yes. That I can imagine, but quite frankly, Sister, I know that you're not one of them. That's why I'm curious about who wrought the change in you. I don't imagine you've always been like this. Crusading women usually look like battleaxes. And even that first day when you threw that parcel at me and told me to keep my hands off Lin—what's her name?'

'Kim,' she corrected coldly. 'Kim Barclay. And you really don't have to go to such lengths to convince me that you don't know her. If you lay it on any thicker I might just get the idea you're trying too hard.'

'Don't *you* try *me* too hard, sweetie.' Now he spoke with a threat in his voice. 'For a long time I've been looking forward to letting you know about my cousin Jonathan.'

'Oh yes, I suspect whatever problem he has runs in the family.'

'And what exactly is that supposed to mean?'

Hana shrugged. 'Exactly what you think it means. After all, even before we had met officially I had been told on every side just what a lad Jake was. You have all the nurses eating out of your hand, so it seems, positively fainting with longing for you.'

'Jealous?' The question seemed to offer him a certain perverse pleasure.

'Not in the least.' She actually managed to smile. 'At least I have the satisfaction of knowing what a damp squib all the fabled Jake Carlyon sex appeal turned out to be. Experienced, but dull, that might be my assessment.' Warming to her theme now Hana threw caution to the winds. 'Ten out of ten for effort but lacks real flair.' Her eyebrows rose mockingly. 'Do you think that would be a fair and unbiased report?'

'You're too late, Sister.' He grinned but there was no humour in his expression. 'Just a few minutes too late, it might just as well be half a lifetime. You see,' he traced her jawline with the finger that she had found irresistible a moment earlier but she set her teeth, refusing to allow him to see how easy it would be to re-awaken that treacherous reaction, 'your response was quite unmistakable to someone with any experience of women . . .'

'And of course that means you,' she spat the words at him.

'If you like. But to return to what I was saying, you can talk about damp squibs as much as you like, you can even mention dullness and lack of flair. But those words were far from your mind when I kissed you a moment ago. You might be able to kid yourself but you can't convince me that you didn't enjoy the experience.' Abruptly his hand dropped from her cheek, his smile fading with equal suddenness. 'You show signs of frustration, Sister Dean, and if you're not careful you'll wake up one day to find yourself with nothing in your life but work. You should try to relax more, there's nothing puts a man off more than a female who's got a chip on her shoulder about male/female relationships.'

'Thank you for your diagnosis, Doctor.' Irony made her voice harsh. 'When life gets too much for me, I'll come running to you for help.' The ill-chosen words were out before she had the chance to stop them.

'I'd rather you didn't. I don't mind making the diagnosis but I'd rather you find someone else who will be willing to provide the treatment.'

'Would you please drive me home.' Misery threatened to overwhelm her and she averted her eyes, staring blindly ahead through the windscreen.

'With pleasure.' A moment later they were gliding away from the parking place and the remainder of the journey was accomplished in silence. He pulled up at the gate of Rose Cottage and before he had time to get out and open the door for her she was standing with her hand on the latch of the gate.

'Will you be all right?' She told herself that she was a fool to imagine the faint regret she heard in his voice, ignored the slight softening in his manner towards her as he got out and stood looking down at her.

'All right?' It was nice to realise that she had managed to inject the right amount of scorn into her brief laugh. 'Of course I shall. You don't think that just because you and I have had some words that I shall lie tossing and turning, unable to sleep? I shall be perfectly all right. But thank you for asking.'

'I wondered if perhaps you minded going into the house late at night, that's all. Some women do.'

'I'm sure you have lots of experience of the women who like to have their hands held while they fit the key into the lock, Mr Carlyon. But I assure you I'm not one of the shrinking kind. Goodnight.' And without waiting for a reply she walked swiftly up the path, the sound of her high heels making an insistent tattoo in her brain. Her finger had touched the hall light switch before she heard the car roar away from the kerb and at once her shoulders sagged miserably.

'Oh, Oscar.' Her voice trembled as she bent down to stroke the silky body of the cat as he jumped down from the shelf above the storage heater and rubbed himself against her legs. 'Oscar.' Impulsively she lifted him, ignoring his protesting call and held him against her cheek. 'What a damned fool I am. Now why did I have to go out of my way to make an intolerable situation worse? Can you tell me that, puss?' And to encourage an answer her fingers tightened about him so that he spat and sprang out of her fingers with another indignant miaow. Hana watched him push open the door of the kitchen and stalk across the blue and white tiled floor, his orange tail swishing angrily from side to side. And that seemed to her the final rejection.

Next thing she knew she was running upstairs sobbing noisily. It was just like old times she thought as she lay in her bed allowing the tears to slide down her cheeks and soak into her pillow. She hadn't felt so unhappy since leaving London. Why she thought wildly, hadn't she thought that John might in fact be Jon? Why hadn't Kim Barclay told her?

CHAPTER FOUR

THE days settled down to a certain tolerable monotony, a monotony which Hana welcomed after the crisis of her departure from London and her unhappy start in Bridgestead. She even found that she could look at Jake Carlyon without the awful dislike that had affected their relations when she had imagined him to be Kim Barclay's seducer.

And now that she knew differently she couldn't begin to imagine how she had ever thought so. Not that it was impossible for her to visualise Kim falling for him. No, that was only too easy to understand. Time and again she heard the younger nurses talking about him, and almost always telling each other that he would only have to crook his little finger . . . But somehow she knew that Jake Carlyon would demand a great deal more from his girl-friends than Kim would have been able to offer.

But . . . She had to qualify that thought as she remembered Tanya Catenby. According to what she had heard from Mary, Jake and Tanya saw a great deal of each other and Tanya hadn't exactly impressed with her intellectual qualities that night at the dinner party. Glossy and sophisticated she might be, but she didn't quite fit into the rôle of lifelong companion to Jake Carlyon.

Only, when her imagination took her that far along a track, Hana pulled herself up short. Who says he's looking for anything as permanent as that? she asked herself. It's quite likely that he's more than happy with the status quo. Who wouldn't be, with an apparently endless selection of attractive young women at his beck and call? But then another idea occurred to her. Wasn't James Catenby an extremely wealthy man? Tanya therefore must have the added allure which money inevitably confers.

In spite of her distrust of Jake Carlyon she couldn't quite see him as being on the look-out for a rich wife, but you never knew with men. The pain twisted inside her again. She, least of all, had any claim on understanding them. Look at Lindsay, she reminded herself. And look at the blind way she had put herself in the wrong with Jake. Even now the recollection made her shudder.

But, to do him justice, since the night of Mary's party when the knives had been out between them with such vengeance, his manner towards her had been impeccable. Even that first embarrassing encounter on the Monday morning had gone so smoothly that she found the paralysing apprehension fade in the face of his totally matter-of-fact attitude.

Of course, it had helped that he came accompanied by Dr Jordan and Dr Aziz and that he seemed in a particularly relaxed, easy-going mood during which he wisecracked with the patients in the way they loved.

'For Gawd's sake, Doc, don't make me laugh.' One middle-aged patient recovering from a hernia pressed his hand to his wound and closed his eyes pleadingly. 'It only hurts when I laugh.'

'Oh, they all say that, Mr Thomas.' Jake handed back the chart from the foot of the bed, glancing at Hana as he did so. 'I think we'll have the stitches out tomorrow, Sister, don't you agree?' And without waiting for an answer he moved on to the next bed.

And then, instead of leaving the ward with a brief nod as he usually did, he turned to Hana, demanding in a tone that was only half-mocking, 'Why is it, Sister, that this is the only ward where we're not offered coffee in the mornings?' The glance at his assistants was mischievous. 'And we used always to say that in Fleming you got the best coffee in Bridgestead, isn't that right, Staff Nurse Frost?'

To Hana's surprise the other woman blushed and giggled. Staff Frost who was normally so self-contained and remote actually *giggled*.

'That's right. You did, Mr Carlyon.'

A nod from Hana sent Staff Nurse bustling out to the kitchen and she returned only a few moments later carrying a neatly laid tray with a pot of steaming coffee, sugar, milk and four cups. Calmly, although that was the last emotion she was experiencing, Hana began to fill the cups, stopping the older woman as she turned to leave the office. 'You've forgotten one cup, Staff. Surely you have time to drink a cup with us.'

'Oh. Thank you, Sister.' And when the other cup had been produced the five of them sat discussing the next batch of patients who were due in for surgery during the week. There was one point when Hana, becoming enthusiastic about a new treatment she had seen tried out with some success in London, forgot her inhibitions and began to describe the procedure in some detail.

Her manner became more confident, her voice warmer, more fluent, and she used her hands to give additional point to the argument she was using. 'I'm not saying it's invariably the best way, but Sir Andrew Macintosh thought it was an improvement on the conventional treatment.' Suddenly she remembered who she was talking to, felt her face colour a little and became conscious of Jake Carlyon's intense stare. Nervously she flicked her eyes in his direction, waiting for the cutting remark she was sure would follow.

'Mmm.' There was a frown of concentration between

his eyebrows as his keen dark eyes considered her enthusiasm. 'Yes, I've been reading an article on that. We'll try it!' Swiftly, decisively, he got up, gathering his papers as he did so. 'You're the expert, Sister, so I trust you to put it into effect, explain it so that your nurses know exactly what they're doing. You're lucky to have such an efficient second in command as Staff Frost. She'll be invaluable in helping you.' And with a flurry of coat tails he had gone, Dr Jordan and Dr Aziz following in his wake like tug boats fussing round the ocean-going liner, but not before Dave Jordan had rolled his eyes in comical exasperation.

After that Hana found life became easier all round. Since he seemed prepared to forget what had happened between them she could easily do the same. She was even grateful to him for making it possible. It wasn't every senior consultant who would have been so accommodating. There was more than one nurse in the London who had been forced to move on simply because of a difference of opinion with one of the medical staff—it was all to easy for them to take advantage of their power and influence.

Staff Nurse Frost too had mellowed a bit, just as Mary had promised she would. And without being able to pinpoint the change Hana put it down to Jake Carlyon's approving words that day when she had spoken of the new treatment—certainly Frost put her heart and soul into ensuring that the junior nurses understood what the treatment demanded. It would have been nice to think that the staff nurse now accepted the fact that Hana's appointment had been made solely on merit, but she thought it was probably more to do with Jake Carlyon. He seemed to have the ability of making people jump through hoops for him.

It was a month after Mary's dinner party when Hana,

quite out of the blue, had a telephone call which surprised her.

'Hello, Hana . . .' The voice was smoother and more friendly than she remembered, 'it's Tanya Catenby.'

'Oh, hello.' It was difficult to keep the surprise from her voice while her thoughts were busy trying to imagine the reason for the call.

'It's about our garden fête . . .'

'Oh yes.'

'For the hospital.' Tanya laughed. 'Don't tell me you haven't heard about it?'

'Well, I think someone did say something.'

'Anyway, it's our turn this year. Daddy's just been appointed chairman of the Friends' Committee, Friends of the Hospital, and we thought that we'd try to do something different. Usually we have the fête in the hospital grounds, but this year we thought we might have it at Uplands.'

'I see.' Hana had heard from Mary of the huge country house which the Catenbys had moved into just a few years before.

'Naturally each ward is expected to help. I wonder if you would care to be responsible for one of the stalls. We have a marvellous lot of helpers from the town, of course, but I think it's only right that the hospital should be involved too.'

'Yes, I do see.' Although she spoke quietly there was something patronising about the other girl's manner which Hana found intensely irritating. This, she decided, was probably one of the unseen snags about coming to a small town. At least in London they had been spared contacts with all the do-gooders trying to enhance their already exalted reputations. 'What would you like me to do. That is,' she quickly modified, 'so long as I'm not on duty.'

'I don't think you are.' There was a rustle of paper as Tanya seemed to consult a list. 'Matron kindly let me have a complete copy of the duty rotas and I think you're free on Saturday the 18th of this month.'

'Yes.' It was hard to explain her reluctance so she injected a shade more enthusiasm into her voice. 'I'll help in any way I can.'

'How sweet of you,' Tanya said gushingly. 'And especially when you're so busy all week, all that hard work on the ward. Well, I wonder if you'll be very kind and do either the Coconut Shy or the Bran Tub.'

'The Coconut Shy? But surely that would be best done by a man.'

'Maybe you're right. Then shall we say the Bran Tub? I've told my Ladies Committee to try to collect as many small things as possible but I know you'll be a wonder at begging things from your friends. Well thank you, Hana, that's a great help. Oh and of course we'll supply the Bran Tub. Goodbye.'

The moment Hana put down the telephone she could have kicked herself. Why hadn't she invented an important engagement which would take her away that weekend? Why hadn't she said she was having visitors? Why hadn't she thought of some excuse to absolve her from such a chore? How on earth was she going to collect the hundreds of small gifts suitable for the Bran Tub?

But Hana need not have thought that she was the only one to have been trapped by Tanya's unexpected summons to help at the fête for when she went into the Sisters' Rest Room next morning she found it buzzing with half-exasperated, half-amused complaints.

'What has she nobbled you for, Dean?' Janet Sagan, the fifteen-stone sister in Maternity seemed to relish her part as Madame Rosa, Bridgestead's Only True Astrologer and Necromancer.

'Oh, the Bran Tub.' Hana smiled down at the cheerful face of Sagan, surely the most placid person she had ever met in her life. 'I think it was the only job Tanya had left.'

'Tanya is it?' Sister Wallace looked up from her magazine. 'Nice to be so well in with the people who matter. How do you manage it, Dean? After all, you've been here only five minutes.'

'Oh I met them at Mary Bishop's one night. Mr Catenby is a friend of her husband.'

'I see.' Placidly Wallace returned to her short story. 'Well, don't keep name dropping or you'll make us all jealous.'

'Don't mind her. She doesn't mean a word of it.' Sagan grimaced at the lowered head of her colleague. 'But while we're on the subject of the fête, Dean, can I put your name down for the hockey game we have on the morning of the fête?'

'Hockey? But it's still summer.'

'Oh, we're not purists here, dear.' Fishing in the capacious pocket of her blue uniform Sister Sagan produced a list and began to write down Hana's name. 'Good.' She looked up with a smile. 'I just need one more volunteer. Sure you won't change your mind, Wallace?' She winked at Hana. 'It might be your last chance.'

'No, I don't think I will.' Wallace didn't take her eyes from the printed page. 'Thanks just the same. I plan to do something pleasant like have my appendix removed that day.'

'Who are we playing?'

'Oh, don't you know about it?' Sagan put her list in her pocket. 'It's just a bit of fun really. Almost a hospital tradition. It started to give the patients a bit of a laugh and then someone had the bright idea of running a book on the outcome, not just on the result but on the number of goals scored. And you know they make quite a lot of money. Last year it came to more than three hundred pounds. And don't forget,' she made her stately way towards the door, 'on the day, there are no rules whatsoever. If we can't win by fair means we do our best by foul.' She paused, looking comically anxious. 'I hope you're not keen on the game? As a game, I mean.'

'As a matter of fact I am.' Hana couldn't help laughing. 'What about practice?'

'Oh we don't bother about that.' Sagan flipped a hand through the air dismissively.

'And positions?' Hana insisted.

'Oh, positions. Anywhere you like so long as you don't want to play in goal. I'm afraid I insist on that position for myself. It's difficult for anyone to get past me, you see.' And with that she went out closing the door behind her.

'But who are we playing?' Hana yelled the question in amused frustration.

'Oh, has she gone?' Wallace put down her magazine and stood up with a little sigh. 'You're playing the doctors, Dean dear.' Yawning she stretched luxuriously. 'That's what it is, seven a side, doctors versus the nurses. And you just need a big rugby man like Jake Carlyon charging you and,' she grimaced and rubbed her shoulder nostalgically, 'all you want to do is surrender.'

And that, thought Hana as she braked violently, skidding on the damp turf and just managing to evade a not too gentle tackle from one of the doctors' team, was no exaggeration. But before she had time to reflect on the matter, from the corner of her eye she caught sight of another figure, easily recognisable because of his height, streaking towards her, clearly determined to relieve her of the ball nestling at the crook of her stick.

She took off, racing for the goal which at that moment was surprisingly ill-defended, walloping the ball with all the strength of her arm as she went along. Behind her the thud of running feet made the adrenalin flow even more excitingly, a glance over her shoulder told her that Jake Carlyon was almost on her.

Making a sudden daring decision she changed direction abruptly, capturing the ball with an apparently careless sweep of her stick and having the satisfaction of hearing a muttered imprecation as the force of his speed carried him a yard or two beyond her. And before he had time to reposition himself, Hana, to the enthusiastic cheers of the spectators who had come along to support the game, drove the ball hard with her stick into the back of the net, scoring the first goal for her side.

'Good shot, Sister.' Jake Carlyon's laconic acknowledgement as he ran past her up the field made her heart beat a little faster and gave her the confidence as the game progressed to indulge in the unorthodox play which seemed to be a feature of the game. It was an irresistible opportunity towards the end of the match to hook her stick round another when it seemed that a goal for the opposition was imminent and she told herself that she hadn't been aware that Jake Carlyon was her adversary until he turned round with a frown and a grin which didn't fade even when he recognised his assailant.

But in spite of all that she and her team-mates could do, the result of the match was never in doubt and the only satisfaction that could be gleaned was in the narrowness of the victory for the doctors. As they trooped off the field, Hana heard her name and turned round to smile in response to Sister Sagan's congratulations.

'Well played, Hana.' The use of her Christian name

was a major sign of approbation from the senior sister. 'That goal was a great breakthrough.'

'To me as well.' She was breathless and glowing, not even caring that Jake Carlyon was walking from the field with Sagan. 'But I enjoyed it.'

'She cost us more than that one goal.' Jake's eyes lingered over Hana's face as she waited so they could walk off together. 'You may not have noticed, Sister, but she perpetrated a foul which robbed me of another.'

'A foul.' Sister Sagan was shocked. 'But I can't believe it was deliberate.'

'Of course it wasn't.' Hana felt more light-hearted than she had done for a long time. 'How could you even suggest such a thing?'

'There, I told you. She's much too young and innocent-looking to do things like that.' And catching sight of one of her friends standing on the side lines, Sister Sagan strode off and left them.

The words, so innocently spoken, lingered in the air after she had gone and Hana found herself blushing at his raised eyebrow, the deliberately cynical expression, so that she turned in relief when Mary, with Ted and Nicky in tow, came across and carried them both off towards the tent where coffee and biscuits were laid on. And for the few minutes when they stood drinking and chatting she and Jake Carlyon didn't even have to look at each other.

It was the same for the fête which was taking place in the afternoon. Hana told herself that she was glad not to keep bumping into him all the time. Although that didn't stop her searching for his taller than average figure among all the crowds who thronged round the stalls set round the lawns at Uplands. It seemed that the entire population of Bridgestead had taken the road out of town that afternoon and it wasn't long before the Bran

Tub, which had had a continuous queue of children, was completely sold out.

'Come on, Hana.' Mary who had been helping on the cake stall came up and slipped an arm round Hana's waist. 'There's no point in us hanging about here, let's go into the paddock, that's where all the side shows are.'

As they wandered across, constantly stopping so that Hana could be introduced to this or that well-known citizen, she felt a touch on her arm and looked up startled into the smiling face of James Catenby.

'I thought it was you, Hana. Mary.' He included her in his greeting. 'And you're both looking very attractive if I may say so.'

'Of course you may,' Mary grinned mockingly. 'We . . . or at least,' she qualified, 'I, am not so used to hearing compliments that I'm likely to ban the habit.'

'We is all right.' Hana's smile was more restrained. 'That goes for both of us then.'

'I don't believe it.' James Catenby's eyes had a calculating expression as they looked at Hana then with another few casual remarks he turned away from them to speak to someone else.

'Well,' as they continued across the soft grass, Mary spoke softly, 'what do you think of our local Lothario? I haven't had a chance to ask you.'

'Lothario? Do you mean James Catenby?'

'Who else?'

'Well, he's certainly charming.'

'Oh, he's that,' Mary spoke drily.

'A bit too charming do you mean?' Hana laughed. 'Well you meet people like that. Especially handsome middle-aged men. I suppose it's something to do with the fact that he's both of those things. Men like that don't like to think they're losing their powers over the opposite sex.

'And is he?' Mary slipped in the question with an apologetic smile. 'Do you find him attractive.'

'Well, he doesn't set my pulses racing if that's what you mean.' Hana looked round at her friend questioningly. 'Are you trying to tell me something?'

'Well, tell me to mind my own business.' For a moment Mary refused to look at Hana. 'But Ted was passing your cottage last week and happened to notice James's car at your door.'

'His car? Mr *Catenby's* car do you mean?'

'Yes. On Wednesday evening. Ted and Jake had been playing golf and . . .'

'On Wednesday evening I was out.' Hana felt a shade of stiffness in her voice. 'I went to the pictures with Dave Jordan as a matter of fact.'

'Sorry, Hana. I should have known better. Only, I felt a bit guilty knowing you had met him at our house. I should have warned you that he had an eye for a pretty girl.'

'Well, you needn't worry, love. As far as I'm concerned I haven't spoken to him since your party and even if I had been at home on Wednesday I would not have been in the mood to embark on an *affaire* with him.'

'You don't mind my saying?' It was obvious that Mary regretted having introduced the subject.

'Of course not.' Hana forced herself to laugh. 'But set your mind at rest. I don't really go for married men. What on earth did Ted think of me?' And Jake Carlyon she added dumbly.

'Ted wasn't thinking anything about it. Just said he had seen his car at your door. That's the worst of having a number incorporating your initials. It's difficult to keep your movements secret. Anyway, I've said my piece even if I do feel a fool about it. Now let's go and have our fortunes told.' She slipped a conciliatory hand into Hana's arm squeezing it warmly. 'I'm just dying to hear what Fate has in store for me. Aren't you?'

'I would be if I didn't know who was playing the part of Gipsy Bridget Malone.'

'I don't want to hear.' Mockingly Mary put her hands over her ears. 'I prefer my illusions. And I have complete faith in what she's going to say to me. It's a powerful combination after all. A gipsy *and* Irish. She's bound to have the second sight.'

'Gift of the gab more likely.' But in spite of her scepticism, Hana made no resistance as her friend hurried her across the paddock towards the old-fashioned gipsy waggon which was lending a great deal of authenticity to Sister Sagan's performance.

They didn't have long to wait and while Mary was inside Hana talked in a desultory fashion to the woman who was standing beside her and looked about her at the crowds who were flocking round all the stalls and side shows. Once she caught sight of a tall figure in the distance but before she had the chance of discovering whether or not it was Jake Carlyon the sound of beads rattling distracted her and she turned to see Mary, pink cheeked and bright-eyed, emerging from the caravan.

'Your turn now.' Mary held aside the curtain of brilliant tawdry beads and winked at Hana as she passed into the dimly lighted interior. 'I'll keep my fingers crossed for a tall handsome stranger for you.'

Coming out into the brilliant sunlight ten minutes later Hana saw Jake Carlyon before anyone else which must have been the reason for the swift rush of colour into her cheeks. If she could have avoided him she would have done so but because he was speaking to Mary that was impossible. Besides Ted and Nick were there too, all obviously waiting for her and that first glance told her escape was impossible.

'Come on, love. Tell us what she said.' As Hana joined them Ted draped a casual friendly arm about her shoulder. 'Mary refuses to let us into the secret, you won't be such a spoil-sport, will you?'

'Won't I?' Hana tried to respond lightly, flicking a glance from Ted to Mary but deliberately ignoring Jake Carlyon, conscious as she was of his powerful, slightly narrowed scrutiny. 'I tell you what, Ted.' Flirtatiously she slipped her hand through his arm. 'You go and have your fortune told. It isn't an exclusively feminine diversion after all. Then we can all compare notes.'

Ted wasn't the least bit chastened by the laughter from the other two. 'I might just do that.' His amused eyes surveyed her closely. 'I'd give a lot to find out what brought that blush to your cheeks. Wouldn't you, Jake?'

Unable to go on ignoring him Hana felt her eyes drawn inevitably to the intense gaze that had not left her face since she emerged from the caravan but before Jake Carlyon had time to reply the attention of the Bishops was diverted by some friends who passed just then. And looking at him, Hana had the strangest sensation. She had the sudden impression, no, more than that, the certainty, that he knew exactly what Gipsy Bridget Malone alias Sister Sagan had said in there.

And from that point it needed only a flick of recollection. Sister Sagan lived on the Clyston Road and when her car had been out of action last week, of course wonderful Jake Carlyon had been glad to act as chauffeur. Suddenly Hana's eyes were telling him quite unmistakably what he could go and do with himself.

CHAPTER FIVE

FROM the narrowing of his expression she knew that he had got the message. There was the faintest edge of regret that this was how it must always be with them. A few weeks' tranquillity, guarded approval of one for the other, and then, some little thing would come along to disturb the new-found evenness of their relationship.

Needless to say it all went back to Lindsay. All the insecurity she felt in her dealings with men went back to him. Even though she had pulled herself out of the trough of despondency, she would never again be the woman she had been. Unexpectedly, tears stung her eyes. She felt her mouth quiver as all the unfairness swept over her in a wave.

'Hana.' His voice was low, intimate, as if he understood something of her distress and was reaching out to help her. She wrenched her eyes from his, saw with something approaching panic his hand come out towards her, 'I was going to ask you if . . .'

But before he could finish what he had been about to say, they were interrupted, his gesture towards her was halted by long slender fingers entwining themselves in his. Tanya's voice was sultry as she spoke, leaning against him to let him know how hard she had been working.

'Darling, I've been looking for you everywhere.'

'Hello.' Watching, Hana saw how his expression softened as he looked down at the girl. And certainly, today in a dress that was the same deep violet as her eyes and with her dark hair a cloud about her shoulders, she would have melted the stoniest heart. Add to that the petiteness which must make a man like Mr Carlyon feel absurdly protective, the way that she was hanging on to his every word. It was enough to make you sick, decided Hana as she half-turned, looking round for Mary.

'Oh, Sister.' Tanya relinquished her hold on Jake's arm. 'I haven't thanked you yet for doing such a *super* job with the Bran Tub.' Her smile was easy and practised. 'I've been round most of the stalls and was surprised that you had sold out so early in the day.'

'I enjoyed doing it.' Hana forced herself to be calm. 'And there was a queue even before the fête opened. That probably explains why we sold out before some of the others.'

'Of course. We've had the most marvellous day and I think we're going to break all records. Most of the stalls have done miles better than last year.' She paused before asking the question Hana knew was hovering on her lips. 'Have you any idea about your final figure?'

'I think we're just a bit up on last year's Bran Tub.' Hana's tone was cool, not in the least apologetic.

'Well,' Tanya's determination to hide her disappointment was just a bit overdone. 'Well, thank you anyway, Sister.'

'But wasn't it cheaper this year than last?' Jake's comment surprised both women, although it was Tanya's expression which revealed most. 'I heard on the grapevine that this year the Bran Tub was offering better value than ever before.'

'Really.' There was some tension in the set smile on Tanya's lips. 'And what exactly do you mean by the grapevine, darling?'

'I refuse to reveal my source,' Jake teased. 'But you have my word for it that it was impeccable. The person who gave me his considered opinion insisted that it was the best Bran Tub he had known.'

'It was me, Uncle Jake, wasn't it?' Nick had detached himself from his parents, slipped one hand beguilingly into the man's grinning up at him. 'I told you to try the Bran Tub. I got this.' From his shirt pocket he pulled out a notebook and pencil. 'And Jimmy Ingram got two toy soldiers. That's really what I wanted.'

'Well,' Tanya considered, 'next year we must really decide these things in committee. Try to get as much money as we can for the various things. Don't you agree, Sister?'

'Mm.' Deliberately non-committal, Hana wrenched her eyes from that small but somehow powerful hand resting on Jake Carlyon's arm. It was hard to explain why she found the sight of it so distasteful. 'You must remember, Miss Catenby,' she almost enjoyed the iciness in her voice, 'that all the things were given for the Bran Tub. As I suspect they were on all of the stalls, so whatever money is raised is clear profit. And I really think it pays to be generous with the children. Otherwise,' she flicked a glance in Tanya's direction, finding herself agreeably surprised at the annoyance she recognised on the other woman's expression, 'otherwise you might find that you've lost next year's customers.' And with that she turned quite deliberately and rather rudely away.

It was only a few minutes later that Mary, slightly out of breath, came hurrying up to her, apologising for deserting her for so long. 'They are clients of Ted's and it's difficult to get away sometimes. But in any case I wasn't too sorry when I saw you and Jake having that little chat together. Well, what did you say to him? Did you say yes? Because if you did then you must come out with us.'

'Say yes?' The look Hana turned on her friend was puzzled. 'Say yes to what?'

'Oh?' The change in Mary's expression betrayed her disappointment. 'That means he didn't ask you. I wondered if Tanya had turned up too soon.'

Remembering the words he had spoken before Tanya joined them Hana had just time to regret her own sharpness which had probably delayed his message a little. 'I just don't know what all this is about.' In her ears the laugh sounded light and amused.

'Oh, it's about the do Jake is having at his house tonight. He always asks a few of us back to his place on the evening of the fête. And while you were in having your fortune read he asked me if I thought you would like to go.'

'Oh, what a pity.' The defensive lie came easily to her lips. 'I have something arranged for this evening.'

'Oh, Hana. And it will be such fun.' Mary waited but when Hana showed no sign of explaining exactly what she was doing that night she gave a little sigh. 'But if you can't . . .'

'No. Sorry.' Hana kept seeing Tanya's long pink-tinted nails against Jake's jacket and was unable to think of a satisfactory excuse at that moment.

'Well, tell me,' Mary dismissed what seemed to be an unprofitable topic of conversation for something more promising, 'what did the gipsy see in your future?'

'Oh, the usual kind of thing.' It was difficult to pretend that she didn't notice Mary's keen eyes on her face, doubtless taking in every degree of heightened colour. She laughed uneasily, 'The same kind of thing she told you, I expect.'

'I hope not.' Now it was Mary's turn to blush. 'For she told me that I could expect the patter of tiny feet in about six months time.'

'Mary . . .' Hana stopped and swung round to look at her friend. 'Do you mean . . .'

'Of course it didn't take much second sight for Gipsy Bridget to produce that one from the crystal ball. Especially as she would no doubt have seen the result of the test I had done last week and . . .'

'Oh, Mary.' Impulsively, Hana put an arm round her friend's shoulder and hugged her. 'I'm so pleased. That is,' she hesitated, 'if you are. You and Ted.'

'Of course we're pleased. We always meant to have at least two and with Nicky off at nursery school now . . . That's not to say,' her sidelong glance was just a bit sheepish, 'that the whole thing was planned. It just more or less happened. But we're really glad it did.'

'And Nicky? What does he think about it all? He must be thrilled at the idea of a little brother or sister.'

'We haven't told him yet. We thought we'd like to keep it to ourselves for the first two months and that would have been impossible if we had told Nicky right away. Besides, it's such a long time for a child to have to wait. Actually, you're the first person I've told, apart from the parents.'

'I feel flattered. And if there's anything I can do . . . I must get out some knitting needles and try to knit some bootees or something. It's not exactly my strong suit but . . .'

'Thanks, Hana. That makes two of us. Nicky had some weird and wonderful things to wear when he was a baby but I had sweated blood over them and was determined he shouldn't have a deprived childhood. Anyway, that's enough of what the gipsy told me. You're being very cagey about what she said to you.'

'As I said, the usual thing. She probably has two spiels, one for the married ladies of the parish, another for the spinsters.'

'I doubt it. Mrs Shepheard was two ahead of me in the queue and I don't think my news would please her at her time of life. Besides which she's been a widow for the best part of twenty years.'

This remark caused both girls a fit of the giggles before Mary brought them back to the topic of most interest. 'Come on, then. Or I'll think it was too awful to tell.'

'Oh, she said that there's a tall handsome man lurking somewhere in the bushes who's about to sweep me off my feet.'

'Interesting.' They paused as they reached a corner where the wide drive swept round to the rear of the house and turned to retrace their steps to where the crowds were still ambulating gently about the stalls. 'Look.' Mary pointed to where children were having pony rides. 'I think I can see Ted. There, do you see? He's just lifted Nicky onto that one.'

'Yes. Shall we go back in that direction?'

But they stood without moving, enjoying the pleasant warmth of the afternoon, the colourful scene as women in pretty dresses, men in slacks and shirts, children in shorts and tee shirts licked ices as they wandered from stall to stall.

'I wonder who she could have had in mind?' Mary asked mysteriously.

'What?'

'Old Sagan. I wonder who she could have had in mind for you?'

'Old Sagan now? When all the time you've been insisting on Gipsy Bridget Malone.'

'Well, you must admit she's right on the ball. She couldn't have been more accurate as far as I'm concerned.'

'Of course. I admit it all. For you she was exactly right.

But then she doesn't know as much about me as she does of you.'

'I wonder.' Mary's slow, thoughtful tone caught Hana's attention and, following the direction of her eyes, she found herself looking at Jake Carlyon who was walking slowly towards them. Tanya still had her hand through his arm and his head bent slightly in her direction told them he was absorbed by what she was saying.

'You wonder what?' The words were out before she could stop them, causing instant regret as she knew that anything Mary said was bound to make uncomfortable hearing.

'I just wonder,' Mary's voice was just a shade reticent, as if uncertain how her teasing would be received. 'It seems to me there is the very man who might have been made specially to fit in with the description. Tall,' lightheartedly she considered. 'Yes. And dark. No-one could deny Jake is dark.'

'No, even I couldn't deny that.' Hana decided that the only attitude to adopt was casual amused indifference and her tone seemed to be just about right.

'And handsome,' Mary went on. '*Everyone* thinks he's handsome.'

'Especially Jake Carlyon.' She knew she was being bitchy and enjoyed the feeling.

'Oh, Hana.' Mary was genuinely disappointed with her friend. 'How can you say that? I can't think of a man who has less conceit than Jake.'

'Oh, come off it. Do you think he doesn't know how all the young nurses pant after him?'

'And not just the young ones. There's more than one well into her fifties who becomes quite dewy-eyed at the sight of him. But no, Hana. I won't allow you to say he's conceited.'

'All right. All right. He's the most modest man I've ever met. Does that please you?'

'No.' Mary was being hard to please. 'That's not true either. Anyway I can't stand self-effacing people. No.' As she reverted to her theme she was thoughtful. 'He's just about tailor-made for the gipsy's prediction. Perfect in every way I should say. And nurses make perfect wives for doctors. Don't they?' She grinned, not realising how her casual words were like a knife turning in Hana's breast.

'Do they?' With an effort she hid her feelings. 'I would have thought you'd be the very last person to say that. Besides,' her eyes returned to the couple still sauntering towards them, 'Mr Carlyon gives the impression of being very much out of circulation.'

'Well, I shouldn't let Tanya's proprietorial manner fool you, love. I can't see dear Tanya being the one to turn him into a married man.'

'Oh, I don't know.' Now she felt she was turning the knife in her own wound without any help from Mary. 'She has a lot going for her. She might be just the kind of wife for an ambitious surgeon. Well connected, Daddy chairman of the hospital committee.' In spite of herself a note of bitterness had crept into her voice.

'I don't know that Jake is so ambitious.' Hana missed the curious glance darted in her direction, all her attention was concentrated on the pretty dark girl in the violet dress. 'Not to the extent of taking a wife to help his career.'

'Don't you think so? You would be surprised how many men can fall in love where the advantage lies. Besides,' she recovered herself quickly, 'she's really a very pretty girl.'

'Ye . . . es.' Mary nodded slowly. 'She's pretty. But I somehow think she would get further with Jake if she wasn't quite so clinging. Some men lap that kind of thing up. But I doubt that Jake will be one of them. And I don't think that Tanya's the least bit helpless. Do you?' Mary lowered her voice as the couple drew close. 'She's been around a bit too. That's another thing that Jake wouldn't like.'

'A man's world.' Hana was cool. 'Surely that makes two of them. What's sauce for the goose . . .'

'But it doesn't work like that.' Mary smiled as Jake stopped beside them, releasing himself from Tanya's possessive touch.

But even when she wasn't in actual physical contact with Jake, Tanya had the persistence of a limpet and didn't let him out of earshot. And the glance she sent in Hana's direction, in spite of the sheer beauty of her violet eyes, was a clear warning. Keep off, Hana was being firmly told, he's mine.

As if, thought Hana as she returned the look with coldness, as if she would ever be prepared to fight for him even, and in view of their relationship the idea was almost laughable, even if she *did* find him attractive. She allowed her eyes to rest on his relaxed easy form as he half-turned from the group to exchange some amiable remark with a man who was clearly an ex-patient. Oh, she wasn't so silly as to deny that he was attractive, just that she did not find him so.

Again she became aware of the power of Tanya's animosity but refused to give her the satisfaction of acknowledging it, preferring to detach herself from the group, to lose herself in the crowds who were now beginning to drift away from Uplands. She had had enough of the smug self-satisfaction of the people who had organised the affair. All she wanted now was to go home and put her feet up. What on earth was she doing here anyway, adding to Tanya Catenby's self-importance after a gruelling week on the wards? She would go home and have a long wallow in a warm bath, supper on a tray in front of the television and an early night.

Twenty minutes later she was driving out of the impressive stone gates which lay at the end of the drive, turning right along the road leading to Bridgestead. And yet she didn't feel quite as relieved to be shaking herself free from the people she left behind her as she ought to have done. Mary, for instance, had not troubled to hide her disappointment.

'Hana. Can't you wait just a bit?' Her quick look round had not immediately been able to pinpoint Jake Carlyon's position although Tanya, in the centre of a group of admirers, was only a yard or two distant. 'I *know* that Jake wants to speak to you about his party.'

'Oh well, then, maybe you would explain to him.' Although she forced herself to speak casually, Hana could not disguise her agitation from herself. She smiled artificially, 'I must go. Goodbye, Mary.'

'But, Hana . . .'

Luckily it was possible for her to bend down so she could pretend not to hear her friend's anxious wail. 'Goodbye, Nicky. See you soon.' She whispered. 'And if you can persuade Mummy to bring you up to the cottage some time next week, I'm almost certain I can find one or two of those toy soldiers that dropped out of my box.'

'Hana,' he cried in ecstasy and before any more could be said she had waved a casual hand in Ted's direction and hurried across to the car park.

She kept strictly to the plan she had drawn up for herself, letting out an indignant Oscar who clearly thought he had been confined to his basket on the porch for an inordinate length of time. After all, the swish of his orange tail reproached her, it is a Saturday and I'm entitled to a certain amount of companionship.

Hana followed him along the flagstoned path which led through the garden at the rear of the cottage, neatly bisecting the lawn and disappearing behind the tool shed. She smiled as she watched him spring onto the lid covering the compost heap and from there straight onto the shed roof, his usual look-out point for any unwary birds, then sighed as she retraced her steps towards the house. Cats, unlike people, weren't supposed to suffer from loneliness and if she hadn't known about a party she was missing she wouldn't have been lonely either.

After a bath she felt better and even sang softly to herself as she moved about the kitchen, bringing together the ingredients for the simple supper she was planning. Feeling that this was a time for self-indulgence she had squeezed out the last few drops of bath oil from an expensive bottle her mother had brought from Germany on her last trip and now was enjoying the scent of Je Reviens in her nostrils. And it had seemed pointless to dress properly so she had slipped on a frilly cotton negligee over a short nightie, ignoring the fact that it was hardly eight o'clock and still bright daylight.

A flick of the radio switch filled the room with the strains of the Blue Danube and she remembered with pleasure it was the night for Baker's Dozen on Radio Four so she turned the volume up a bit, humming in time to the music as she spooned some cottage cheese onto a plate and sliced a tomato. She was just turning to the back door in search of some chives when a loud knocking from that direction startled her. She hesitated, thinking not for the first time that the cottage *was* slightly isolated, then with a shrug at her own foolishness, turned the handle and pulled the door open.

She felt Oscar rub himself against her legs, heard his indignant miaow as if he had been shut out in the snow for hours, but both those sensations were overwhelmed by the shock of seeing Jake Carlyon filling the entire doorway. His eyes seemed even darker than usual and there was a flicker of something like anger as they swept over her, noting every single thing about her, from the tumble of fair hair round her shoulders, to slim feet clad in flat gold thongs. Confused, Hana bent to pick up the cat from the floor, cuddled him against her breast while she tried to appear wholly at ease.

'Doc . . . Dr Carlyon.' The stammer made her blush and her mind went vacant again. While he stared at her with that blend of irritation and condescension it would be impossible for her to think of anything.

'May I come in?' He was as cool and controlled as ever. Despite the eyes.

'Of course.' Even deeper colour flooded her cheeks, she turned away, glad of the excuse to hide it from him, heard him follow her and close the door very firmly behind him.

They were trained to notice, to observe, and Hana was very certain that he was doing just that even if he appeared to be looking only at her. She was aware of the glass of milk on the tray, the meagre portion of cheese, the sliced tomato. The silence seemed to stretch endlessly until she felt her confidence begin to flow back. 'Won't you sit down?' She indicated one of the chairs pulled close to the table.

'No thanks.' He paused, while his eyes continued their merciless enquiry. Hana felt irritation begin to overtake her earlier feelings. How dare this man force himself into her home, acting so very much the great man where he had no rights? Surely she was entitled to a little time to herself, free from the demands of the hospital Gods.

Her chin rose slightly, the light of battle appeared in her eyes.

'I had to come this way on my way home.'

In a split second Hana's mind covered a great distance. On his way home. But surely the direct way from Uplands to Clyston was via Uppington. This was *one* route but not the most direct. She frowned with the effort of concentration.

'And I decided to come in and check that you had had my invitation.' He continued without pause, 'I'm never happy about doing these things through other people.'

'Invitation?' Hana procrastinated.

'Yes.' His tone was dry, a faint smile softened the irritation she had deciphered earlier. 'Invitation, Sister. I understood Mary had told you I would like you to come along to my house tonight. I always have a party on the evening of the fête and most of the senior staff come along.'

'Oh, that invitation,' she said foolishly.

'That one,' he agreed equably, then paused. 'My mother looks forward to meeting people from the hospital.'

'Your mother?' Her tone showed a tactless astonishment.

'Yes, Sister.' From his tone she could not say whether or not he was displeased, or amused perhaps, but he did subside so that he was leaning against the corner of the table and their eyes were pretty much on a level. 'Contrary to what I'm sure you believe,' he paused and, still keeping his attention firmly fixed on her face, his hands reached out for the cat she was still holding. As he took Oscar from her nerveless grasp, his hands brushed against the curve of her breast, making her—and him no doubt—aware of how very little she had on, 'I *do* have one. Like other people.'

'I'm sorry.' How could she concentrate on what he was saying when that sensitive accidental intimacy had set all her emotions jangling.

'I was telling you, Sister,' surely now he was laughing at her, jeering even, 'that I too have a mother. I'm not *so* unusual.'

Suddenly everything he had said was in her mind, causing her to blush furiously but also to smile ruefully. 'A likely story, Doctor.' And she was pleased, irrationally pleased for such a little thing, when he laughed with her.

'Well,' his amusement died quickly, his eyes were fixed on hers again, 'What do you say, will you come along about nine?' He spared a swift glance at his watch, eased himself away from the table and deposited Oscar on the floor.

'I . . . I . . .' Feeling trapped Hana tried to recall what she had told Mary. 'I was feeling rather tired. I promised myself an early night.'

'Oh,' he said blandly, 'and here was I imagining you had a very exciting date. I wonder where I got that idea. I even went so far as to check that young Jordan was on duty tonight.'

Colour flamed in Hana's cheeks at the realisation that he knew she and Dave had been seeing a bit of each other, but before she could think of a polite way of telling him to mind his own business he went on. And this time she sensed that he was trying, quite deliberately, to warn her.

'You know, Sister, I don't think you should push your luck *too* far. I think I've been more than patient with you considering the circumstances of our meeting.' The eyes that raked her now were full of menace. 'And although I might give the impression of being mild and easy-going,' when he paused this time he could have been giving her the chance to show some scepticism but she was scarcely in the mood for that, 'I can sometimes be extremely awkward.'

'I'm sure you can.' It was irresistible and she was pleased when she saw his eyebrows come together, surprised when he smiled faintly.

'At least we understand each other.'

'So, the . . . suggestion is,' she frowned as if she were trying to get it straight, 'I've to come to your house tonight or you'll make it awkward for me at the hospital, is that right, Doctor?'

'I'm glad you got it.' He looked at his watch again and smiled at her amiably. 'So, we'll look forward to seeing you about nine, then. I must dash, I'm sorry.' He spoke as if she had been persuading him to dally a little, then paused with his hand on the door knob. 'But really, Sister,' he seemed determined to rub salt in her wound, looking with satisfaction into her mutinous face, 'You'll have to think of better excuses after this. I'm not one to accept vague explanations of a previous engagement.'

'No?' Her eyes narrowed as she looked at this man who seemed so determined to remind her of past unhappiness. 'Is it so strange that I should be going out with someone?' Teeth bit against her lower lip.

There was a strange expression on his face as he stood there, half-turned from her but with his eyes fixed on her mouth. 'No, Hana,' the sound of her name on his lips brought a tremor to the base of her spine. 'Quite the reverse in fact.' Unexpectedly he took a step towards her, his hands came out and touched her face, cupping it for a moment before trickling down till they circled her neck. Blood pounded in her veins as she stared up at him. 'It was the vagueness I meant.' His voice was distractingly gentle. 'There will be nothing vague about your relationships with men.' A second later the door had closed quietly behind him. She was deprived of his touch, left with all the unfulfilled longings which had been such a torment after Lindsay. Why, oh why should they be returning now with such devastating power? Just when she had decided they were firmly under control.

CHAPTER SIX

THE only thing to do was to enjoy the party. So she consoled herself as she parked her car along with all the others on the wide circle in front of Dene House. But that decision couldn't quite control the nervous way her stomach was churning as she walked up the flight of steps to the front door, nor chase from her mind the picture of her last unfortunate visit.

'Ah, Hana.' Before she could pull the heavy brass ring, Jake appeared from a door at the back of the large hall, coming towards her with a welcoming smile in which there was a touch of sardonic amusement. 'I'm glad you could come.'

'It was so kind of you to *invite* me,' she said sweetly as she allowed herself to be led across an expanse of deep blue carpet.

'You look . . . nice.' A touch on her arm held her back at the door. 'I suppose you know that.' His eyes were serious, all trace of derision had vanished from his voice. 'Beautiful, in fact.'

'Thank you.' It must have been nerves that made tears come suddenly into her eyes so that she was forced to bite her lips and look down.

'Hana, I . . .' But before he could say any more there was the sound of footsteps and a couple, apologising for being late, came into the hall.

'Hana,' still there was a look of concern about his face as he began the introductions but Hana regained control immediately and the smile she turned on the middle-aged couple was dazzling. 'This is May Findlay and Bill.

He's the village doctor here and why he of all people should be late I don't know. Talk about a sinecure! Hana Dean is a new sister at the hospital, she's come up from London and has been able to throw a lot of valuable light on some new developments. Now, I must see about getting some drinks for you people.'

For a few minutes Hana found herself absorbed into the crowd about the door but she noticed that the guests, many of whom were from the hospital, had spilled from the large drawing room into the garden. Most of the people there were already known to her and inevitably much of the conversation centred on the day's events. To her surprise Jake didn't leave her for long and soon she found herself being led over to an elderly woman sitting on one side of the fireplace which glowed with polished brass and an extravagant arrangement of dahlias in the grate.

'Mother, this is Sister Dean, I've told you about her.' What, Hana wondered with a little shiver, did that mean exactly? 'Hana, this is my mother, Lady Colville.'

In spite of anything she might have heard, Lady Colville showed no sign of reluctance to meet her son's new colleague, quite the reverse in fact for she smiled as she held out her hand, then ordered her son to bring a chair so that Hana would not have to stoop to speak to her.

'I've been having this trouble with my joints, you see. That's why I couldn't come to the fête this afternoon.' Hana gave an appreciative smile at Jake as she sat down, then returned her attention to the woman. 'I came down specially from Edinburgh to attend it and then my son forbids me to go. And it seems to have been such a success.' She looked beyond Hana towards the other guests. 'Tanya was telling me they hope to be up about fifty per cent on last year. Where has she gone?'

'Yes, it was a huge success.' Damn Tanya Catenby, Hana thought as she smiled. 'You've come down from Edinburgh, did you say?'

'Yes, Henry, my husband, is professor of rheumatology at the university, but at the moment he's in America doing some research. I should have gone with him but because of this flare-up I changed my mind at the last minute.' She smiled. 'I don't know if it's unlucky or lucky that I should be married to an expert on my complaint. I'm waiting for a hip operation now.'

'Well, they're very successful, you'll know that.'

'Of course they are. The trouble is I was a nurse myself. I married Jake's father during the war when I was a QA, an army nurse, you know. He was in the medical corps and was killed in Korea when Jake was just two years old . . .'

'Oh.' This was the first Hana had heard of Jake Carlyon's early history. 'How awful for you.'

'Mm.' There was pain on the older woman's face. 'Such a waste . . . for everyone. But it seemed inevitable that Jake should be a doctor too. I don't think he ever considered anything else. Then, when he came to Bridgestead, we bought this house down here in Clyston,' her eyes twinkled with mischief, 'and he made the mistake of bringing a senior colleague home for lunch one day.' Her eyes moved upwards from Hana's face, telling the girl that her son had rejoined them. 'I'm telling Hana, you don't mind me calling you that, my dear, about how you got your mother off your hands. It should have been the other way about.'

Almost unwillingly Hana glanced up at Jake just in time to see Tanya slip her hand into his arm and smile sweetly down at his mother. Totally ignoring Hana, of course. 'What should have been the other way about, Lady Colville?'

How she loved that title, Hana thought, as she looked at the glowing face. How satisfying it would be to marry the son of Lady Colville, to have your picture in the *Tatler* or the *London Illustrated*.

'I'm saying that Jake found a husband for me when the natural thing would have been for me to look for a wife for him.'

'Mother.' He was smiling fondly at her with a shade of exasperation. 'I'm quite capable of finding my own wife.'

Tanya sighed and looked up into his face with death-less devotion. 'I'm sure you are.' And her ripple of laughter made Hana feel quite sick.

It was a relief when at that exact moment a woman came into the room—Hana at once knew her as the woman she had met at the gate that first day and pray-ed, successfully it seemed, not to be recognised. She announced that the meal was ready and would everyone please come through to the dining-room. Hana found herself between Mary and Ted whom she had scarcely spoken to so far and Mary was deter-mined to discover the reason for Hana's presence in view of her earlier insistence on a previous engage-ment.

At first Hana's inclination was to deflect the questions but the sight of Tanya, just a step in front of them, was too tempting to resist. Especially when she gave the impression that she was more interested in the conversa-tion behind her than the one she was engaged in. She glanced round, straight through Hana, who found her irritation increasing.

'Oh, there are times,' she spoke archly, a little loudly so that Tanya wouldn't have to strain too much to hear, 'when I *do* allow myself to be persuaded.'

'I see.' Mary looked intrigued as they drew closer to

the laden table. 'And let me guess, who did the persuading?'

'No need to guess,' Hana laughed in what she hoped was a mysterious way. 'It was Jake. He stopped on his way back from the fête.'

'Really.' Mary seemed oblivious of the daggers Tanya was throwing in their direction. 'And was he so persuasive that you finally cancelled your other important date?'

'That's all I'm prepared to say.' Her tone implied there was a great deal more that could be said and she had the satisfaction of seeing Tanya who had almost reached the dining-table flounce away as if she had suddenly lost all taste for food.

'Well, let's see what she makes of that.' There was an air of satisfaction about Mary as she helped herself to some cold ham, deliberated over the varied selection of salads.

'Wh . . . what do you mean?'

'Oh come off it, Hana.' Mary raised an eyebrow and pushed a large plate at her friend. 'Don't tell me that wasn't all put on for Tanya's benefit.'

Hana smiled wryly. 'Am I as transparent as all that?'

'No. Just to another woman. She affects me like that too. Makes me feel really bitchy and I want to scratch. I suppose it's jealousy. She's rich, beautiful.' She sighed mournfully and put a morsel of green pepper into her mouth. 'Men seem to flock round her like flies about the honey. Even Ted . . . and he should know better.'

'Oh, Mary,' Hana couldn't help laughing. 'That's nonsense and you know it.'

'I do know.' With an abrupt change of mood Mary grinned. 'I'm just testing. Seeing how it would feel if he were really keen on Tanya. On the other hand, I wouldn't guarantee what would happen if she did flutter her lashes invitingly in his direction.'

'You know exactly what he would do. He would feel flattered and turn with relief to you. He would see that you were warm and pretty and that you had charm and . . .'

'And patience and efficiency,' added Mary.

'Yes, those,' Hana agreed. 'And modesty.'

'Of course.' Both of them burst out laughing and Ted, who had been talking to someone else, turned back towards them.

'What's so funny?' He looked up and took the glass of sparkling wine which Jake was offering. 'I'm asking just what they're laughing at.'

'Yes, that's what's intriguing me too.' He cast a swift searching look towards first Mary, then, more unhurriedly, in Hana's direction as he supplied them with drinks. 'See if you can keep it for a moment, Ted, I'll come right back.'

And when he did, it was to guide the party in the direction of the garden, joining some of the other guests who were sitting at the clusters of small tables dotted about the paving outside the french windows. 'Now,' when they had found chairs and pulled them round a vacant table so they could eat in some comfort, he looked up at them, 'you can tell Ted and me what you were laughing at.'

'Oh,' Mary widened her eyes teasingly at him, 'I've quite forgotten, haven't you, Hana?'

'Forgotten?' As she pulled her features into an expression of perplexity Hana dabbed at her mouth with a serviette. 'Forgotten what?'

Then they both started to laugh again while the men exchanged long-suffering looks before transferring attention to their food. But by then Mary and Hana, assisted no doubt by the wine, had only to look at each other in order to be overtaken by a fit of the giggles.

'You know what, Ted,' Jake leaned back, one hand casually draped over the back of his chair, the other toying with the stem of his glass, 'if I didn't know we were in the company of two responsible ward sisters, I would get the idea that we had picked up two bird-brains on Blackpool pier.' There was a tolerant expression on his face, a curve at his mouth, and Hana couldn't ignore the fact that he seemed constantly to be seeking her eyes.

'I know what you mean, Jake.' Soberly Ted collected their plates and cutlery, 'I think we'd better go and bring some pudding for them. It doesn't look as if they're fit to go themselves.'

'Yes, I am.' When she wanted to Mary could move quickly and now she practically jumped to her feet. 'You two sit still, we'll get the dessert. Will you trust me to choose for you, Hana?'

'Yes, of course.' Hana tried to hide her dismay at the idea of being left alone with Jake, but from the faint twist at his lips she was certain she had not succeeded.

'I'll just have cheese, Mary,' he said easily, then, when the other two departed he continued to sit back in his chair, studying his guest as if she were a particularly interesting patient at one of his clinics.

She was the one who spoke first and then it was more in desperation than in a desire to make polite conversation. 'It's been a lovely day.' She stretched to try to indicate how much she felt at ease.

'Yes.' His sigh was sheer contentment. 'It's not often we're as lucky as this. Even now,' he looked up at the sky with its slip of moon just visible behind one of the great trees bordering the property, 'it's more like midsummer than the end of September. I can't imagine when we last had such a warm spell so late in the year.'

Just then Mary and Ted returned and Hana was forced to choose between a meringue with raspberry sauce and a slice of gooey-looking chocolate cake which she decided to have.

'Heavenly.' When she had finished she sat back and patted her trim waist. 'I adore all chocolate puddings. But tomorrow I shan't eat at all, to make up for tonight.'

'That I absolutely forbid.' Jake pushed back his chair. 'Come on, Hana, our turn to do the work. We'll bring the coffee, shall we?' And Hana felt she had no choice in the matter. But instead of going directly towards the house a touch on her arm guided her down a few steps. 'Let's go round the garden, shall we? I always think it's best at this time of night.'

All the sounds of the party drifted away from them as they walked along the path; the night enclosed them in a world of soft velvety magic. On one side of the path were wide herbaceous borders with trained fruit trees, heavy with apples and pears against the high brick wall while in the centre was a large rectangular lawn immaculately cut and with sharp edges, the faint moonlight casting vague shadows over everything.

'Mind.' He stooped to lift back a trailing branch so that she could pass easily. Then, as they walked down towards the end wall, she heard him strike a match, turned to see him light his pipe then glance up at her in the split second before the flame guttered and went out.

Hana felt that throb of passion again, the one that had been so hard to understand back at the cottage, and was suddenly breathless. In her lungs she felt the spicy scent of the tobacco as it drifted towards her and she knew that he was still looking at her. They were less than a foot apart, two yards from the spot where she had first seen him. Remembrance stretched between them, separating, pulling together.

Then something soft and light came towards them over the lawn, a shape that materialised into Tanya whose powerful exotic perfume overwhelmed the more subtle scents of garden and smoke. With a murmur of irritation Jake pulled the pipe from his mouth and pushed it into his pocket.

'Jake.' It was hardly a reproach. 'Daddy's just arrived and I've been looking for you everywhere. They said you had come to show off your garden.' Her laugh tinkled out. 'What do you think of it, Sister Dean?' She slipped her arm through Jake's, Hana sensed rather than saw her fingers reach down beneath his cuff where she could touch his skin with her soft hands.

'Oh, it's beautiful. I thought so last time I was here.' She hadn't meant to say that, it just sort of slipped out, but it gave her again the feeling of satisfaction that was becoming such a compensation in her dealings with Tanya. 'But really I must go. We were supposed to be getting coffee for Mary and Ted.' And she turned and walked swiftly across the grass.

Behind her she thought she heard a gasp. Tanya showing her reaction, she supposed. But, less pleasingly, she imagined tightened lips from Jake and hoped she wouldn't have to pay too high a price for that moment's satisfaction. She had almost reached the edge of the terrace when, behind her, she heard an exclamation of anger, swiftly but barely controlled.

'Damn.' Even when she was using a low voice Tanya could sound shrill. 'Damn it, something caught at my tights. I'm sure they'll be utterly ruined.' Hana felt almost light-hearted as she ran up the few steps.

She was crossing the hall, carrying a small tray with five cups of coffee, Tanya would probably come back to the table with Jake and there was no sense in being *too* pointed, when from a group in the shadow of the staircase a dark figure detached himself and she found her way barred by James Catenby.

'Hana.' He had a deep melodious voice of which she sensed he was very proud. 'I'm delighted to see you, my dear. I didn't have a chance this afternoon.' Masterfully he took the tray from her and indicated that she should go ahead of him. 'Lead on and I'll bring this for you.'

'Hasn't Mrs Catenby come with you?' Hana asked as she threaded her way through the sitting-room towards the garden and hoped he would take her point.

'No, she rarely does come out in the evenings.' He sighed bravely. 'It's a great pity, I have to go to so many functions and I *need* someone to help me.'

'Oh, well,' Hana said briskly as if she were speaking to a patient who needed consolation, 'I'm sure your daughter is always willing to step in.'

He was a very smooth operator, Hana had to admit it. Charming, distinguished-looking and not too obvious. In fact he gave most of his attention to Ted during the time they sat together at the table in the garden and was able to join them in a cup of coffee as Jake and Tanya were occupied elsewhere. But from time to time he looked across at Hana with an expression that seemed to hold a distinct invitation.

He was too perfect, she thought with calm detachment. That thick white hair which contrasted so strikingly with the suntan. Surely that must be acquired only by spending hours under a sun lamp? He had overdone it only a little, it bordered on the vulgar and so did the way he kept talking about his daily squash games, an implication that he was the best in the district, as if he were determined to emphasise his virility. And talk of sport was how he was offered the opportunity to focus his attention on Hana once again.

'You didn't see the hockey game this morning, then, James?' Ted leaned back in his chair, replete, just a little more expansive than usual.

'No, I was kept pretty busy at Uplands.'

'Oh, you missed the best game for years. And the star was the person sitting opposite you.'

'Really?' The dark eyes dwelt on her as if he had discovered some absorbing interest. 'You surprise me. Though,' he gave a short laugh, 'why I should say that I don't know. It's obvious you're a bit athletic the way you move.'

'Yes, Hana scored two of the goals for the nurses. She had them running round in circles, the doctors I mean.'

'Well! We'll have to get you along to the squash club. Do you play, Hana?'

'I have played. When I was in London. But I don't think . . .'

'Nonsense.' He looked briefly at Mary, 'Why don't you bring her along with you one day, Mary? To one of your women's games?'

'Well, I don't think I'll be going till . . .'

'I really don't think I will.' Mary and Hana spoke at the same time, but it was Hana who continued with a smooth determination. 'I don't feel I have the time at the moment. I work fairly long hours at the hospital and then the cottage and garden take up most of my free time. I'm afraid,' she smiled across at him, 'squash will have to wait till I get my life more organised.' Then she rubbed her hands down her arms and shivered a little, 'If you'll excuse me, I think I'll go to the car and get a stole, I'm just beginning to find it a bit cool on my arms.'

When she came back with her shawl over her arm, Hana took advantage of the cloakroom on the ground floor to go and repair her make-up, to check that her hair wasn't too untidy. She was lucky to have the room to herself and took the opportunity to study herself with more detachment than she had been able to summon before she left home.

She had been right to stick to the simple, in a more elaborate dress she would have felt conspicuous. As it was the shirtwaister dress could hardly have been plainer in style, but the gorgeous softness of the material made it drape beautifully against her figure without clinging. And the colour, a stunning vibrant green to which changing light brought a bluey sheen, did wonderful things to her hair and skin tones.

Tonight it seemed the flecks of gold in her brown eyes were brighter than ever and her long lashes were a perfect frame. Her slightly wide lips wanted another touch of apricot gloss, a swift comb through her hair and she was satisfied. She picked the wispy shawl, a soft thing in a blend of blue, green and pink, from the chair and turned to go, only to find her way barred by Tanya Catenby who came whirling through the door, evidence of temper pulling down the corners of her mouth.

For a moment she simply glared, her eyes sweeping from the top of Hana's head to the tips of her toes, then, with an expression of boredom, she turned away. Without saying a word, Hana walked to the door but before she could pull it open the other girl's voice stopped her.

'I suppose,' Tanya's voice was distorted as she stretched her lips to apply some gloss, 'you realise that it was simply because I persuaded him that Jake asked you along here this evening.'

Hana didn't reply but stood staring at the glass where Tanya was admiring her reflection.

'Yes.' It was a nice smile, showing perfect white teeth even though it seemed not to reach the violet eyes.

Satisfied with what she saw, Tanya turned to face the other girl. 'I did want *everyone* who helped at the fête in *whatever* capacity.' Her tone indicated what she thought of Bran Tub officials. 'And it would have looked so *odd* if only one person had been absent.' She had an irritating habit of emphasising every other word. And her laugh was irritating too. 'I think everyone knows that you and Jake don't see exactly eye to eye. Even,' she wrinkled her short nose while the dazzling eyes were particularly watchful, 'even if they have no idea what it's all about.'

'And what,' Hana felt suddenly chilled, 'what is it all about?' Was it possible that Jake had discussed it all with her, had he told her of Hana's unexpectedly avenging appearance on his doorstep, had they laughed about it together? Now her skin was burning hot. Maybe she had asked for it, telling Tanya that she had been here before. It was clear enough that the other girl wasn't likely to rest until she had discovered the reason for that visit to Dene House. She tried to concentrate on what Tanya was saying, clenched her hands against her sides, determined to control her rising temper as the laugh gurgled again.

'Oh there's no need to go into that,' Tanya said meaningfully, but there was a shade of relief in her eyes as someone pushed at the door and one of the other women guests came in.

'I've come to collect my jacket.' The newcomer looked from one of the girls to the other, almost as if she sensed the atmosphere between them. 'People are beginning to go home. It's been a marvellous day, I expect you're feeling quite pleased with yourself, my dear.' She smiled at Tanya.

'Of course,' Tanya gushed. 'I'm absolutely *delighted* and I've had so *many* willing helpers.'

'And what about Molly? Wasn't she able to come?'

'No,' Tanya sighed. 'You know how she is. Going

through this bad spell. Something to do with her age I suppose but I feel *so* sorry for poor Daddy. He's . . .'

Hana, closing the door firmly behind her, missed the rest of the conversation and stood for a few moments in the hall, unobserved by the half-dozen people standing about having a last chat before they separated for the night. Then a kind of panic overcame her. She couldn't bear to hang about any longer. Apart from anything else she was exhausted. Playing a wild game of hockey in the morning, supervising a bran tub in the afternoon then madly coming to a party at night. It was just too much and she'd better get home before she flaked out completely.

She murmured a few words to Mary and Ted who were standing by the door of the drawing room and looked round frantically for her host so she could say goodbye. Then her attention was drawn to Lady Colville who had moved from her original position and was just saying goodbye to two of the guests.

It was a relief to know that she could avoid the son completely by thanking the mother so she went over to Lady Colville and bent down, taking the free chair one of the women vacated.

'Oh, are you going?' The older woman looked quite disappointed. 'We haven't had the chance to talk.'

'I'm sorry about that.' Hana smiled. 'Each time I looked you seemed to be surrounded by friends.'

'That's true. You see, I know so many people down here.' She was a bit apologetic. 'But it's nice to catch up again on all the local news. Only I would have liked more time to speak with you, my dear. Jake has told me a lot about you.'

'About me?' In spite of all the control she could muster Hana felt colour stain her cheeks. He had spoken about her to everyone it seemed, and probably little to her credit. 'Oh dear!' Further comment she dare not risk.

'I'm always interested in new staff at the hospital. And it was such a terrible thing when poor Jean Elgin was killed. But I heard you've coped very efficiently in Fleming.'

'It's kind of you to say so but I'm still trying to find my feet.'

'Ah well, you'll soon get over that, my dear, and feel you've been here all your life. I wonder where Jake has got to?' She looked about the room. 'I saw him a moment ago with Tanya. But they both appear to have disappeared.'

'I don't know. I was looking for him. But perhaps you would say goodnight for me, Lady Colville. I've had a lovely time. It was so kind of him to invite me.'

'Nonsense, my dear.' The dark eyes gleamed for a moment. 'I would have thought it rather strange if my son had not asked you. He's always had an eye for a pretty girl.'

'Oh . . .' Hana blushed again, annoyingly, then decided it was time to make the final break. 'Well, I really must go. It's been so nice to meet you. Goodnight.' And a few moments later she was fumbling with the door of her car and replying in a synthetically cheerful voice to the farewells of the other guests who were departing about the same time.

She drove home automatically, without really thinking of what she was doing, aware of little but the aching pain in her chest almost as if she had suffered some kind of cardiac arrest. Still, she was too familiar with the feeling to think for a moment that she was a victim of any such thing. Numbly she garaged the car and climbed out, slamming the awkward doors so that the locks engaged properly. The last thing she wanted tonight was to have to get out of bed at four-thirty because the doors were threatening to tear themselves from their hinges. With her kind of luck even a calm night like this could turn itself into a fury of wind and rain, she thought.

She had reached the cottage door when the sweep of blinding headlights caught her and she realised that a car was pulling up at the gate, such a large powerful machine that for a moment her heart was bounding in agitated excitement. Had he been so annoyed at her departure that he had abandoned his guests and . . .

But instantly she caught hold of her imagination. Besides, this car was an entirely different shape. And the silhouette slamming the door, coming in through the gate, was clearly not that of Jake Carlyon. Silver hair gleamed in the faint moonlight.

'Hana,' James Catenby's deep voice confirmed his identity. 'I was just on my way home when I saw you.'

'Oh?' She pushed aside the suspicion that he must have seen her leave and decided to follow her. Instinctively her hand left the key already half-engaged in the lock and turned to him.

'There's something I just thought of . . . when we were at the party, something I've been meaning to have a word about.'

'Oh,' she said again, her mind going back to that time when his car had been seen at the door. 'What was that, Mr Catenby?'

'Can't I come in for a minute?' His voice was full of sophisticated amusement at her reluctance to invite him inside.

'Oh, of course,' she said smoothly and turned the key in the door.

He stepped inside after her while Oscar disappeared through the closing door. 'Hmm.' Coolly he looked round the little hall, noticing the charming old furniture, the crooked stairway which stumbled its way to the upper floor, then he followed Hana into the sitting-room.

'I'm afraid the fire's not on, but if you're cold I can switch on the electric.' Inwardly she sighed, wishing he would go and let her get to bed. Reluctantly she waved him to a seat and sat down herself, but on the edge of her chair.

'It's an attractive little place.' He studied the beamed ceiling as he lay back on the chintz covered sofa. 'But I can appreciate what you said back there, it's too much for you.'

'I don't think I said that.'

'Not in so many words, Hana.' He smiled his professional charming smile. 'But in any case, didn't you say,' he frowned as he tried to remember, 'that you had taken it for just six months. That'll be up soon, I should think.' The dark eyes resting on her slim figure were all approval.

'Yes, almost. But I've been very lucky for Mrs Castle has written to the agent asking if I would like to stay on for another few months. Her son wants her to stay in Australia over Christmas.'

'I see.' Was it possible to decipher a shade of disappointment in his voice?

'And I'm delighted, of course. I love Rose Cottage and I'll even be sorry to leave Oscar.'

'Oscar?' He looked bewildered.

'That was Oscar who slipped past you when you came in. Which reminds me,' pointedly she glanced at the clock on the mantelpiece, 'I must go and let him in before he decides to go mousing over the fields.' There was a short pause. 'I'm still not certain what it was you wanted to speak about, Mr Catenby.'

He frowned pointedly at her formality but smiled as

he took the hint and got to his feet. 'Oh, it was just an idea, Hana.' In spite of his casual manner he was, she realised, extremely watchful. 'You see, I've just completed a block of luxury flats in the town. You've probably seen them, they're overlooking the Victoria Gardens and have an attractive view beyond to the golf course. That part will never be built up so they can only appreciate in value. And as you'll be looking for a place to live . . .'

'Oh, I know them,' Hana smiled in relief, 'but I could never afford to buy at those prices. I've seen them advertised and although I agree that they look most attractive, they're quite beyond my means I'm afraid.'

He laughed with her. 'I wasn't suggesting that you buy one, Hana.' He paused. 'What I was thinking was, I have this plan for hanging onto one of them. As a matter of fact they're all sold except the one I've decided to keep for myself. Naturally, it's the best one, everything in it is top quality, but I'm not in a position to occupy it right now. It's just a quirk of mine, I thought, well when I get older I might not be able to find a smaller place to move into. What could be better, close to the town and the golf course? Anyway, I thought I might let it for a year or two, you know what I mean.'

'And,' Hana spoke very slowly and she never took her eyes off James Catenby's face, 'you're asking if I would like to move in.'

'That's it exactly. It would be fully furnished and I think I can promise it will be very attractive indeed when it's finished. I'm having the whole thing done by professionals with no expense spared. You could even, if you wanted, choose some of them yourself. I can see by the way you look after this place,' he cast a discerning eye round the comfortable sitting-room, 'that you would be an,' he paused and his eyes returned to her face while he spoke the next words with some kind of deliberation, 'ideal tenant.'

'I still feel sure,' Hana felt her lips were stiff but she tried to speak carefully—after all, he was the chairman of the hospital committee—'that the rent would be beyond me. I get Rose Cottage cheaply because I'm on my own and because I look after the cat. Otherwise I'm sure I couldn't afford a furnished place at all. But thank you for the offer.'

'Oh, don't worry about the rent, Hana.' He walked from the sitting-room to the front door, 'I'm probably in the same situation as Mrs Castle, more interested in the kind of person than in the rent. I'm sure,' he paused with his hand on the handle, eyes searching her face for some clue as to her reactions, 'we could come to some mutually satisfactory arrangement.' He pulled the door and the cat brushed past him with a purr of pleasure, springing to his favourite position on the third step from which he was in the habit of surveying life. 'Goodnight, Hana.' He waved a friendly hand before pulling the door closed behind him.

She stood staring at it long after the latch had snapped into position and the powerful car had roared away into the distance. Then she moved to snap off the downstairs lights before wearily climbing the stairs. Oscar rubbed himself against her legs when they reached the top together and stalked ahead of her into the bedroom where he sat unblinking in the old-fashioned nursing chair which was his own private property. Here he passed the nights when Mrs Castle was at home and Hana had had no chance of changing the habits of a lifetime. The yellow eyes surveyed her steadily as she sank onto the stool in front of the dressing table and began to remove her earrings and bracelets.

There was an expression of shock in her eyes now that she was alone. Downstairs, while James Catenby had been with her, she had been able to hide everything she had been feeling. Well, she had had plenty of practice at that. A smile of slightly bitter amusement twisted her lips. She had been propositioned. There was little doubt about it, her visitor had been testing her reactions, very discreetly, of course. Hana stood up, undid the buttons of her dress with a controlled violence, threw off the rest of her clothes and pulled her nightdress over her head. A moment later she was lying in the darkness between cool cotton sheets.

What was the matter with her that a man like James Catenby should think she was fair game? She wasn't going to have her life complicated by the unwelcome advances of a married man. She turned over restlessly and punched the pillow into submission. Not even if he were the chairman of the board. Come to that, *he* would have to be careful. The hospital authorities would not like to think of their senior staff being annoyed by such suggestions. If he became a nuisance she would just have to drop a gentle hint in his direction. But, somehow, she didn't think that would be necessary. Unless she were a much worse judge of character than she believed, he would accept her refusal and turn his attention elsewhere.

Only, his visit, unwelcome as it had been, could hardly avoid directing her thought in that general direction. She gave a sob that was a mingling of despair and self-pity, pulled the pillow against her as if it were a lover. 'Jake.' The name came from her lips in a sob that was an admission of some kind. It was a pain and at the same time a relief, to admit to herself that if Jake Carlyon had been the one to appear at her door with such a proposition, her rejection would not by any means have been so automatic. In all probability, she would not have been lying in this bed alone tonight.

The thought of it was sheer torment, with just a sprinkling of bliss until, somewhere around dawn, she fell asleep.

CHAPTER SEVEN

DEAR Mr Carlyon,

It was so kind of you to invite me to your party on Saturday evening and I would like you to know just how much I enjoyed it. It makes such a difference when you come to an entirely new job to find that your colleagues are so hospitable and friendly. It was also very nice to meet your mother and I hope that soon she will be able to have the operation which should relieve her of much of her pain.

Thank you again for inviting me to your home and for taking me round your lovely garden.

Yours sincerely,

Hana Dean.

That was the letter she had written on Sunday, addressed it to Dene House and posted it in town so that he would be sure to get it on the Monday. In other circumstances she might have used the telephone to express her thanks, but the very idea of encountering him on the line made her even more uptight than she was that day.

By now of course she had calmed down a little and the idea of the note didn't seem quite as brilliant as it had done then. Now she regretted that she hadn't given it more thought, wished she had written less formally, with less desire to be distantly correct, more to express genuine gratitude. After all, it had been kind of him. Both he and his mother had been welcoming. But she knew, by some instinct, that her letter would not please him. And now that his rounds were almost due she felt

116

herself getting all jumpy at the thought of his cool glance at her.

'Are you all right, Sister?' Frost had been all consideration these last few days and when she had been able to give some time to consideration of the change it had made Hana wonder. Last Friday there had been a kind of suppressed excitement about her and she had, most unusually, asked for some time off in the course of the working day.

'I'm fine thanks, Staff.' Hana looked up from the notes concerning the cases the doctors would want to see during their rounds, making an effort to smile. 'Just a bit tired, that's all. It was a hectic weekend and I couldn't seem to get off to sleep last night.' Worrying about facing Jake Carlyon this morning, she reminded herself with a little nervous tremor.

'Oh?' Frost looked slightly crestfallen, hesitated for a minute, then appeared to come to a decision. 'I wonder, Sister, if I could just have a few words with you before the rounds.'

'Of course.' Hana gestured to the chair at the other side of the desk. 'We've plenty of time before they come. What is it, Staff?'

'Well, it's . . .' Staff Nurse Frost swallowed nervously. 'I think I might be leaving, Sister.'

'Leaving?' It was the last thing Hana had expected to hear and most unwelcome news. 'Oh no.'

'Well,' the other woman's face was flushed, 'it's not absolutely certain but I . . . I gave your name as a possible reference. You see, I've applied for another job and at the final interview on Friday,' her colour deepened, 'I know I ought to have told you then that I was going about another job but . . .' She shrugged, 'I thought I might be disappointed again. I couldn't bear everyone to know about it.'

Hana nodded. 'I understand that. I felt just the same when I applied for this job.'

'*You* did?' Frost seemed surprised but she went on. 'The job is as Matron of a private home for the elderly. And I think I'll get it if you and Mr Carlyon will support me. I know Mr Carlyon will, he's told me as much, but . . . If you could see your way to recommending me.'

'Of course I will, Staff Nurse. But I might as well tell you, I would much rather you stayed here. Fleming Ward won't be the same without you.'

'It's kind of you to say that, Sister.' Frost looked down at her fingers locked together in her lap. 'Especially when . . . I wasn't exactly welcoming when you first came.'

'I can understand how you felt, Staff. And I don't blame you. It must be hard to see someone take over what you thought was yours.' A little bleakness entered her features as she remembered how she had thought Lindsay was hers. Until Hester Brownlow came on the scene. 'But I meant what I said, you'll be very much missed in the hospital and especially in Fleming. Sure I can't persuade you to change your mind?'

'I don't think so.' Frost smiled in a way that lightened her slightly severe-looking features. 'You see, there's a flat in the home, quite a nice place with two bedrooms and a large lounge, and I'll be able to have my sister come and stay with me. She works in Taunton and the home is only three miles outside the town so it will all work fairly well. Besides, the salary is high, much more,' she couldn't resist saying, 'than I would get as a sister in hospital.'

'Well, I'm glad for your sake. Although,' Hana sighed, 'we shall all miss you and I can't think of anyone else who will do the job as well as you do. Not half as well. It's going to make my life very difficult.'

'Thanks, Sister. I hope,' Frost coloured again, 'maybe on your day off you would like to come over and see us. It's not such a long drive and Meg would like to meet you.'

'That's kind of you. I'd like that and . . .' But before she could finish what she was meaning to say Hana caught a glimpse of the flurry of white coats turning the corner into the ward and she stood, picking up her notes. And Staff Nurse Frost, only too familiar with the workings of the ward, dashed off to make certain that the nurses had finished their preparations for the doctors' rounds. Hana walked to the door to greet them.

It was Dave Jordan who caught her eye first. He was just a step behind the consultant and Hana knew that his raised eyebrows were meant as a warning. 'He doesn't lose his temper often,' Dave had confided when they had been speaking of his boss, 'but when he does, keep your head down, my girl.'

But that was impossible in this situation and her eyes inevitably met—clashed she decided afterwards might have been a better description—with his. Coolly condescending, he held out a hand for the batch of papers she held.

'Notes, please.' None of the usual niceties, not as much as a good morning. So much, she thought resentfully, for his threat to make things difficult for her if she *didn't* accept his invitation. To show that she was by no means intimidated Hana glared back as she handed over the records.

'Hmm.' He frowned, then walked up the ward with none of his usual banter to the patients, discussing the various cases in an undertone with Dave and Dr Aziz but completely ignoring the Sister who remained a step behind till she was summoned by an angry exclamation.

'Sister!' The very word was a reprimand and he made

sure the whole ward knew it. Fighting the wave of colour
that threatened her cheeks, Hana stepped forward to
where the covers were pulled back from Mr Hogg's leg.
He had been in hospital for a longer time than usual even
for a femur as badly broken as his had been. Most of the
trouble had been caused by the splintering of the bone
which had penetrated the skin in several places, and
excessive contamination from oil and dirt in the garage
where the patient had been working.

Instantly she saw the tell-tale seepage from the wound
discolouring the bandages, but before she had time to
make any comment Jake Carlyon turned scathingly, 'I
thought I had made it clear, Sister, that these dressings
were to be changed frequently.' At least he was keeping
his voice quieter now, but it was even more devastating
in its effect than a moment earlier when he had been
determined to let the whole ward know his low opinion
of the Sister, tinged as it was with acid.

'That is what we have been doing, Mr Carlyon.'
Confidence in her own actions gave her the courage she
needed.

'It doesn't look like it.' The deep-set, intense eyes
were fixed on the frill of her cap, as if he couldn't bring
himself to look at her, then he returned his attention to
the patient, beginning to undo the layers of bandaging as
if none of the nurses could be trusted with their work.
Even while she seethed with anger Hana had to admire
the gentle way he was setting about the job, but before
she could stop herself she answered him, quietly and
with some regard for the patient who was looking in
consternation from the consultant to the Ward Sister.

'I changed the dressings myself just before you came
round. Sir.'

'As often as necessary, I think I said, Sister.' He didn't
spare a glance in her direction. 'If they required chang-

ing again just before my rounds began then that is what
you should have done. I'm not one to stand on cere-
mony,' he said unfairly, 'not where the patients' comfort
is in doubt.'

Hana felt it was safe to play her trump card. 'Have you
looked at Mr Hogg's notes this morning, Mr Carlyon?'

'In due course, Sister.' He frowned as he finally
uncovered the badly scarred leg with its red and weeping
wound, then embarked on a softly-spoken consultation
with his colleagues while Hana bundled the dressings
together and gave them to a passing nurse to dispose of,
signalling that the trolley should be brought to the bed.

She smiled at the patient while from the corner of her
eye she could see Jake Carlyon frown over the notes she
had prepared and felt a tiny surge of triumph that he
would be reading her comments about the overnight
deterioration of Mr Hogg's leg. If you had done as you
usually do, she fumed at him, I would have mentioned it
to you, but no, you had to barge into the ward without
the courtesy of . . .

'I think we'd better have you back in the theatre, Mr
Hogg,' Jake addressed the patient reassuringly. 'Sister
will arrange for you to go down today to have some
X-rays done and we'll see you tomorrow. Got that,
Sister?' He turned an enquiring, detached face towards
her, then swung back to the patient without waiting for
an answer. 'Don't worry. We'll have the leg all right in
the end. It's just been complicated by the circumstances
of the accident.' He smiled reassuringly, murmured a
few more words to his colleagues and went on to the next
patient on the list.

Hana pulled the curtains closed behind them, murmured a few words to Mr Hogg who smiled rather wanly
at her, shrugged his shoulders as if they had both suffered from the consultant's ill-humour.

'I'll get Staff Nurse Frost to wrap you up again, Mr Hogg. Sorry you're having so much to put up with.'

'Thanks, Sister. Now,' he whispered, 'you'd better go. Not often *he's* in a bad mood.'

But it seemed he still hadn't got rid of his temper for the round was punctuated by a series of petty faults which he had found in the nursing care of Fleming Ward on that particular morning. Not that he directed any further comments in Hana's direction. He just let her know that he expected something more than this. Most of his comments were ill-founded, but in one case it was mortifying to find that he was justified in his remarks. A junior nurse had omitted to fill in the temperature chart and no matter how the patient protested that she had been called away when the man in the next bed had slipped and fallen, Jake Carlyon was not in a mood to be appeased.

Quite distinctly Hana heard him murmur something about 'today's nurses' which she took as a direct reflection on herself, but although she glared at him, he didn't turn in her direction. Then he was off, without so much as the customary word of thanks and seeming not to see Staff Nurse Frost carrying the tray of coffee in to the office in preparation for the post-rounds discussion.

'What on earth's wrong with Jake?' Bewildered and obviously disappointed, she followed Hana in and put the tray down on the desk.

'Don't ask me.' Hana controlled her inclination to snap at her deputy. 'He just seems to be in a fiendish humour. And before we have that coffee, I would be glad if you would go and put some fresh dressings on Mr Hogg's leg. I just received a rather public reprimand for neglecting it.'

'Neglecting it?' There was incredulity in the older woman's voice. 'But it's less than an hour since you did it. The poor man has had hardly any peace since last night.'

'Yes, I know,' Hana said grimly. 'But apparently that doesn't satisfy Mr Carlyon.'

'But didn't he read your notes? It says quite clearly that the wound has been discharging since last night.'

'I don't think he read the notes till afterwards.'

'I wonder what's wrong with him?' Frost mused, 'it's not like him to be so nit-picking.'

'Isn't it?' said Hana sourly.

'No, not at all.' Frost sounded quite defensive. 'And I wanted to have a word with him about a reference.'

'Well, maybe you'd better go down to his office and speak to him about that. Go and put the coffee back on the stove till you've done Mr Hogg's leg, then, when you've done that come back and we'll discuss one or two things while we drink the coffee. He had a number of other niggles this morning and,' Hana sounded quite grim, 'I want to make sure that they don't happen again. After that, you can go along to see if you can catch him in his office. And I hope he'll be in a better mood by then.'

But when Hana was alone again in her office she was free to let her anger smoulder. It wasn't altogether the first time she had been in this situation, no ward sister could ever say that the doctors were uniformly reasonable and fair in their dealings with the nursing staff. Some of them were arrogant, with no understanding or interest in the problems of the care of patients. But Jake Carlyon wasn't one of those. Her own experience and his reputation told her as much. But it hurt even more to think he had chosen this way to get back at her, making her look inefficient in front of patients and staff alike. Her anger flared into something stronger, obliterating those softer feelings which she had been harbouring for some time, and suddenly another grievance took shape at the back of her mind.

What was it Frost had said when she had asked Hana for a reference? 'I know Mr Carlyon will support me, he's told me as much.' So, Hana's eyes narrowed as she pondered. That could mean anything. At the moment she chose to think that Jake Carlyon had been encouraging Frost to look for another job. It was easy enough to imagine the kind of conversation that might have taken place between them:

'Yes, Staff, I agree with you, it's most unfair.'

'Not once but twice. Sister Elgin I could understand. Well, she was older than I am—but a much less experienced nurse. From London.'

'Well, there must be plenty of other jobs going. If you feel unhappy with the present set-up then you should look round.'

'Maybe I will. Certainly I don't feel like putting up with the humiliation.'

'That's right, Staff. And if there's anything I can do then don't hesitate. You know I have the highest opinion of you. If I had been here when the interviews were conducted . . .'

'Yes, thank you, sir. I'll remember.'

But when Staff Nurse Frost came back with the coffee, Hana was able to talk normally with her and to thrash out the various problems that had caused so much comment that morning. After all, she reminded herself, she had no quarrel with Frost who would be leaving soon anyway. It was Jake Carlyon whom she had to think about, who seemed intent on undermining her authority on the ward, who was actively encouraging a very efficient staff nurse to desert proper nursing and to go over to what was really social work.

And Frost's report of her reception when she went

along to his office a little later could only confirm what Hana had thought. He had promised to do everything he could to ensure that she got the job she had set her heart on, even to the extent of taking a note of the names of those on the board so he could make direct contact.

'Jake was his usual charming self.' Hana didn't know whether the other woman was deliberately rubbing it in or not. 'So whatever was upsetting him he's got over it. Probably nothing to do with us at all,' she said comfortingly. 'Just that you were unlucky and had to take the brunt of it. But he did say, what is Fleming going to do without you, Staff Nurse?'

Hana bit back her anger. 'Well, isn't that exactly what I said to you myself?'

'Yes, you did.' Staff Nurse Frost sounded a little smug, making it clear to Hana exactly whose comments were valued, whose were of little importance.

In the weeks that followed the atmosphere of hostility between herself and the senior surgeon gradually returned to a kind of armed neutrality, although they never quite reached the guarded friendliness which had been such a pleasant feature of their previous co-existence. Indeed, it was difficult to assure herself that life had ever been that easy.

Frost's departure was marked by a party in the sisters' rest room attended by most of the staff. It was Jake, of course, it always had to be Jake, who made the farewell speech and presented the gifts from her colleagues, a set of crystal glasses and a portable television, and he was also present at the coffee party on Fleming when Hana handed over some gifts on behalf of the ward staff.

On both of these occasions Jake spoke very warmly about the staff nurse and although Hana echoed everything he said, somehow the fact that *he* made the comments she took as a personal affront, a covert admission that if he had not been abroad at a particular time, then they might not be in the position of saying goodbye to such an efficient nurse as Frost.

Through it all Hana had to smile gracefully, though she got her own back by refusing to look at him while he spoke and then deliberately, when she knew she had his slightly sardonic attention, she sent a particularly mean-ing look at Dave. What a bore, her look was meant to imply, having to listen to all this again, but Dave mis-understood, frowned slightly and shrugged, but outside Jake's view.

It was about this time, towards the end of November, when plans were beginning to be made for Christmas that James Catenby swam back into Hana's orbit, albeit briefly. She had seen him once or twice at various functions she had attended and on each occasion he had been perfectly natural in his manner towards her. If anything *she* had been the one who had shown some embarrassment, something which she imagined Jake Carlyon had been aware of. They had both been guests at a cocktail party held by Dr and Mrs Aziz and when she had turned round to find herself unexpectedly facing James and Molly Catenby she had been thrown off guard. And of course that was the very instant when she looked away and saw Jake, lounging against a wall but his eyes very knowingly on her warm features. The intense dark eyes held hers for a short while before dismissing her and returning to what his companion was saying.

And that companion was, of course, of course, the very dishy girl who had come to replace Frost. From her first day on the ward, she had come from Women's Surgical along the corridor, Angie Newcombe had made it clear that she was willing to be friendly with all the doctors but especially with Jake Carlyon whom she appeared to know well enough already. Hana had had no idea that she was on visiting terms with Dr Aziz and wondered if it was possible that Jake had secured the invitation for her.

And if that was so, then what did it say about his friendship with Tanya Catenby? Unconsciously her eyes sought James Catenby as if in his face she could find some answer to her query. Then she blushed as he smiled at her across the room.

Maybe it was this that gave him the encouragement to call again at Rose Cottage. But if so one-thirty in the morning was a funny time to choose. On the other hand it was just possible that his car *had* seized up with a frozen diesel problem, it was certainly cold enough.

The door knocker loudly pulling her back from a deep sleep had been most unwelcome on a bitter November night and when she wakened, heart hammering against her ribs she lay on for a moment, hoping her mind was playing her tricks. Then it came again, so loud and insistent that she knew she hadn't made a mistake. With a groan of protest she switched on the bedlight and reached for her dressing-gown.

'Who is it?' The exterior light switched on showed only the outline of a man through the obscure glass.

'It's me, Hana. James Catenby. I'm sorry to wake you so late but my car's broken down just at your gate.'

'Oh.' She paused with her fingers on the bolt, unwilling even then to open the door.

'Can I use your telephone? Then I'll wait till a recovery van comes.'

For a moment it occurred to Hana to say she would call the garage for him, then the absurdity of the idea made her pull back the bolt without further delay. 'I'm really sorry about this, Hana.' He stepped inside, looking sleek and comfortable in a heavy dark crombie overcoat, his hair gleaming in the soft lamplight in the hallway. 'Disturbing you when you were having your beauty sleep.' His eyes drifted approvingly over the folds of her blue fluffy dressing-gown, making her feel pleased that it covered her warmly from neck to toe.

'That's all right.' She pointed to the tiny recess. 'The telephone's there.'

While she heard him speaking to the all-night garage who promised to pick him up in about ten minutes, Hana debated the wisdom of going into the kitchen to put on a kettle. The last thing she wanted was to have to offer him coffee or tea but she knew she would want a cup herself and there was the matter of refilling her hot water bottle. As she hesitated he put down the telephone and turned towards her with his switch-on smile.

'That's all right.' His eyes swept over her again, this time with a shade more warmth than he had allowed earlier. 'They'll be here before we know it.' He walked towards the door with the air of one who expects to be stopped. 'I'm sorry you were troubled, Hana. I wouldn't have dreamt of it if it hadn't been an emergency. I suppose,' he hesitated with a falsely apologetic little laugh, 'I suppose there's no use hoping you were awake.'

Normally she might have lied but this was hardly a normal occasion so she shivered, 'No, I was sound asleep.' She stifled a yawn.

'Well,' he was determined to smile, 'I can see I'm keeping you. You're getting cold. No central heating?' He looked around. 'Have you thought any more of that suggestion I made?' He raised an eyebrow. 'The flat will be ready just after Christmas.'

'No, I haven't thought of it.' She shivered again. 'I've decided to wait here until Mrs Castle comes back. And I've had no word about when that will be. Besides, I couldn't leave Oscar on his own.' She thought that must be the last word but she had under-rated James Catenby's vanity and persistence.

'Well, I'll have to see what I can do to persuade you. Perhaps we could have a meal some night and discuss the thing properly.'

Ask your wife to give me a ring. The words hovered on Hana's lips but before they could be uttered the sound of an approaching vehicle made him pull the door open and they could see the headlights come up the incline towards the cottage. The cold night air struck through what she was wearing and she shivered again.

'There, I hope you haven't caught cold.' The car seemed to be slowing and he smiled and put out a hand to touch her shoulder at the very moment when the headlights of the car illuminated them with dazzling clarity.

Hana heard a low gear engage as the car almost stopped then a moment later the lights swept over and away from them as the driver accelerated away from the cottage. She had an impression of a long low red car, one that was instantly recognisable even though for the present she refused to admit the identity of the owner.

'It's not mine after all.' There was a shade of smugness about his dark eyes as they seemed to notice her confusion. 'But I won't keep you here any longer, Hana. The garage will be along within a few minutes. I'd better say goodnight and thank you.'

When the door had closed behind him and the bolt was firmly in position, Hana ran upstairs, forgetting the hot water bottle which would be an essential if she were to thaw her frozen feet sufficiently to allow her to get back to sleep again. Oscar's eyes gleamed at her from his chair before she flicked off her lamp with an angry finger. Moments later she heard a vehicle stop, lay in the brightness of the headlights while the men talked on the road outside. Then after about ten minutes she heard two cars start up and drive away, leaving her in the darkness.

Only then did she allow her thoughts to dwell on that split second when she had seen that car flash by her gate. Jake Carlyon's car. Oh there were other dark red Jaguars, there was no doubt about it. But his was the only one she knew. And what could be more appropriate for the pattern that they seemed to have set for themselves that he should just *happen* to pass on the night when James Catenby was at the door. It was almost as if he were spying on her so that he could catch her out, she thought wildly.

And if he had been he would be able to draw some very definite conclusions. The realisation of what those must be made her shiver in a way that had little to do with the cold.

His car at her gate as if it were parked. The only lights in the house the one upstairs, a bedroom light, it would hardly take Sherlock Holmes to reach that conclusion. And the hall light so that the departing visitor could see his way out. And completing the picture, in the background, herself, clearly just out of bed, just as clearly wearing a dressing-gown. With the best will in the world she could hardly blame Jake for arriving at a very natural conclusion.

Despair overwhelmed her, more bitter and painful than any she had known since she had left London. For the rest of the night she lay, sometimes almost drifting off into sleep but always in the end jerking herself awake with a sense of doom oppressing her. Until the alarm went off at six-thirty and she was glad to get up and make herself some tea.

But the last part of the comedy was yet to be played and with unerring instinct fate seemed able to choose the situation which would cause most embarrassment to her. They were having the usual cup of coffee in her office after the rounds when Hana saw a man from the local florist's shop poke his head through the ward door and catch the eye of one of the nurses.

Jake Carlyon was perched on the edge of a small cabinet close to the door and through the glass behind him the delivery man offered the nurse a cellophane-wrapped bunch of flowers. The girl seemed to be expressing surprise but she studied the small card that was nestling among the yellow roses, frowned in mild disbelief smiled a little, then controlled her features when she realised she was being observed. She came forward and tapped on the glass causing Jake Carlyon to swing round so that the door could be opened.

'These are for you, Sister.' Hastily the girl thrust them inside where they were grasped by Jake who stared down at them for a moment before putting them on the cabinet beside him.

'Come then, gentlemen, we are overdue in Jenner.' And without another word to Hana he disappeared, taking his two colleagues with him.

'It looks like you have an admirer, Sister.' Angie rose and walked to the door, sparing a slightly envious glance in the direction of the flowers.

Only when she was alone did Hana rise and go where her curiosity could be satisfied.

'With thanks for last night.' The message was clearly visible for anyone to see. And she was certain that Jake Carlyon had read and understood their import. She turned over the card and saw James Catenby's name engraved on the other side. Ostentatiously, but with a great deal of satisfaction, she took the flowers and, without removing them from their cellophane covering, she dropped them into her waste paper basket.

CHAPTER EIGHT

CHRISTMAS on the wards was always a time Hana enjoyed and this year being on duty was a compensation for the fact that she would be alone during the hours when she wasn't actually at the hospital. There had been talk of her parents and sister coming home from Germany, but that had fallen through and the substitute plan was for Hana to take some leave in the New Year and join them for a ski-ing holiday.

Mary Bishop had been very persistent in her enquiries, but somehow Hana had managed to give the impression that she had had lots of invitations and would be having a hectically social time. To be honest, there were one or two outings planned, one with several of the sisters who had booked a dinner in one of the nearby hotels which opened for the Christmas season. It was advertised as a Boxing Day Party and Hana only hoped she would be in the mood for such a thing. Fond as she had become of her colleagues, she wasn't sure that she had a great deal in common with them once the subject of work had been exhausted.

Of course, there was the hospital dance to look forward to. She had heard a great deal about that from the junior nurses and wished she could match their enthusiasm. They spoke of it as if it were the event of the year and Hana longed to recapture even part of the thrill it had always been in the old days. Even last year . . . Firmly she closed her mind to that, there was no sense in harking back. No matter what Janet Leishman had hinted in her letter earlier this week, there was no question of going back.

It was probably that letter which had had such a devastating effect on her emotions, making her feel so down. Not that Jan had meant it to be like that. Hana was certain that she had slipped in those carefully casual sentences merely as a warning.

'Oh, by the way, love, Lindsay was asking Toby how you were liking Bridgestead. I don't know how he found out where you were. You know it's all off between him and Hester.'

That was all, no comments or opinions, although Hana knew her friend must have been sorely tempted to add some penetrating observation. She was keeping her options open just in case they should get together again. Not, Hana assured herself mournfully, that there was the slightest chance. It was hard for her to explain to herself just why she was so certain of that. But she knew that if Lindsay suddenly appeared and threw himself at her feet, begging her to marry him at once, she would have little difficulty in resisting. And it wasn't *totally* her pride which would stop her. It was just, oh she didn't know, just that she wasn't the girl she had been six months ago.

Unbidden her mind veered in the direction of the morning's rounds, allowing herself a smile of satisfaction at Jake's decision to discharge Mr Hogg. Following the investigation in theatre they found a splinter of wood, a minute thing that hadn't shown on any of the X-rays and which might even have been moving around in the tissue, but once that had been extracted the wound had healed swiftly and he had made rapid progress in gaining the confidence in walking, often such a problem after a fractured femur.

Since the morning when he had gone out of his way to

be so gratuitously unpleasant their relationship had returned, not exactly to normal, but at least he had been formally correct with her, had even once or twice allowed a glimmer of humour to soften their dealings. There had been times when she had been aware of his eyes on her as she went about her duties with the reassuring confidence which the patients found such a comfort and then she had been especially careful to give no cause for adverse comment. If finding some excuse to criticise were indeed the reason for the scrutiny. But what other reason could there be?

On the evening of the dance she arrived home feeling exhausted with what had been a particularly gruelling day in the ward. There had been a multiple accident on the motorway and although the more seriously injured had been taken direct to Plymouth, Bridgestead, in common with the other hospitals in the area, had had their share of those requiring minor surgery. It had happened in the early hours of the morning and the surgeons had been operating for more than twelve hours at a stretch, setting and pinning broken limbs, stitching up superficial face injuries and, in several more serious cases, coping with the internal ruptures which are such a frightening feature of road accidents. But now all the patients were comfortable and barring further complications were expected to make full recoveries, although several of them would be spending longer than just Christmas and New Year in hospital.

Hana pushed open the front door of Rose Cottage with a little sniff of self-pity. On top of everything else she wouldn't be surprised if she were developing a cold. Even Oscar must be feeling the effects of the cold weather for he left his comfortable seat in the kitchen only reluctantly and stood on the doorstep indecisively for a moment before venturing out into the dark.

If it hadn't been for one thing and another she would have stayed at home. Hana knelt in front of the fire and opened up the draught, hoping that a few sticks and small pieces of coal would revive it. She held out her hands in satisfaction as the dry wood sprang into life, feeling a surge of gratitude for the comforts of the little house she had become so fond of. If only she could go and have a bath and curl up on the settee in front of the television. Why go out on such a cold night when you didn't have to? She shivered again before getting up from her knees and answering Oscar's pathetic miaow at the front door, then going into the kitchen to make some tea.

But promptly at nine o'clock she drove the car into the hospital car park and made her way across to the lecture rooms where the dance was always held. She had been listening to the chatter about the event for weeks, hearing all about the fantastic decorations the nurses had been busy with in their free time, so it seemed ungracious to opt out. And, as well, it was expected that the senior staff should attend. Gossip had it that someone had missed promotion because they were too high and mighty to enjoy the annual shindig.

'You're an ambitious young woman, Dean,' Sagan had offered the advice, 'so mind your ps and qs. These things do count. You wouldn't like to miss being Matron just because you didn't come to the Christmas Dance.' She laughed to show that she wasn't being serious. 'Why do you think I go along? It's not because I really believe that all the young doctors are dying to dance with me, though most of them do, bless them. No, it's because I still haven't given up hope yet. Older people than I have been made Matron.'

Obligingly Hana had laughed, concealing from friendly Sister Sagan how her words had sent a cold shiver down her spine. Was that what the future had in store for her? Years and years of getting older in the job, always hoping to get a Matron's position—she wasn't even certain that she would want to be a Matron, divorced from real nursing—worrying when, like Frost, you were passed over for someone else.

Hana studied her reflection in the mirror, wondering if she had been wise to be so extravagant with the eye make-up. This, after all, was Bridgestead, not the West End. And bravado was misplaced, she couldn't even think why the word had come into her mind. Still—she glanced at a chattering group of nurses at the other end of the long mirror who were studying their images devotedly—compared with them she was positively restrained.

Satisfied now with herself, she adjusted the narrow rouleau belt about her waist, a faint smile curved the wide mouth into a happier expression than she had worn for months. In fact, her facial muscles felt stiff with disuse, she must remember that tonight and allow herself to relax.

And that she found fairly easy to do, at least in the short term, for almost as soon as she stepped into the hall, now so attractively decorated as to be scarcely recognisable, she found herself seized by Dave Jordan and swept onto the floor. There was a tiny group on the dais at one end of the room beating out an irresistible rhythm with more power and style than their numbers seemed to justify.

It was so long since she had danced that Hana found it a positive joy to allow the seductive throb to spiral through her veins.

'You should have told me you were good,' Dave's eyes were blatant in their admiration as he gyrated opposite her, clicking his fingers in time to the beat of the music. 'And I would have taken you disco-ing.'

'Oh yes?' She ignored her own breathlessness and smiled at him. 'That doesn't seem a proper pastime for respectable members of the community like us. An up and coming young surgeon and a staid ward sister.'

'Staid you might be most of the time,' he grinned with unflattering frankness, 'but not right at the moment. You know, Hana, you look quite sensational. You'll have all the eyes out on stalks.'

'I hope not.' She turned away from him so that he shouldn't see her blush. She hoped she had been right to choose this dress. But perhaps he was right, it was not the kind of dress to encourage ideas of shrinking modesty. Her shoulders were protected by the narrowest of straps, the bodice fitted her curvy figure snugly and the full skirt ended in handkerchief peaks around her slender calves. Ridiculous heels gave her a few inches in height so that she and Dave were almost on equal terms.

She had a very clear idea of how she looked, her mirror at home had passed on a message and she knew that she had never looked better. The golden brown chiffon of her dress seemed to find a reflection in her eyes and even her skin took warm honey tones from it. Her cold, she reflected inconsequentially, as Dave put his arm about her waist and pulled her close, seemed to have disappeared, probably a figment of her slightly disturbed imagination. The music had changed abruptly from the frankly brash and noisy to the soothing and seductive. It felt pleasant to be held close to a man again, Hana reflected happily. And just at that moment, as they moved round the edge of the dance floor, Hana looked dreamily up and into the eyes of Jake Carlyon.

He allowed his eyes to rest on her for a moment, a long, assessing, faintly cynical look which took in the drift of dark gold hair about her shoulders, the parted, expectant softness of her mouth. Then, before shock had time to register in Hana's eyes, he transferred his attention, now smiling and interested, on the girl who had materialised at his side.

Angie Newcombe had had no thoughts about being overdressed for the occasion, decided Hana with a pang of something like hatred for her staff nurse. She was the kind of girl who would never be prey to self-doubt, which was probably half of her charm. The other half was bound to be her looks for there was nothing un-obtrusive about these. Tall, willowy, ash-blonde hair hanging almost to her waist and those wide blue eyes which she felt sure would be sufficient distraction to any man.

'Well, the kids have quite outdone themselves this year,' Sister Sagan relaxed against one of the chairs round the small table on the edge of the floor where they had a good view of the room. 'I don't think I've ever seen the decorations so nice.'

Hana looked upwards, admiring the slowly moving golden balls, the gay bunches of holly heavy with red berries, trying all the time to pretend that she hadn't noticed Jake Carlyon moving across the room towards them. Her heart was hammering against the thin material of her dress, with such vehemence that she was surprised no-one else had noticed. It was possible, just, that he was coming to ask her to dance. She had seen, with a resentment that could only be explained by their peculiar relationship, that he had danced with all the ward sisters, or nearly all. And with the doctors' wives, oh it was all very correct, in the right order of seniority she decided bitterly. And she supposed that he would feel obliged to ask her. After that, with his duty dances completed, he could devote himself *entirely* to Angie Newcombe who seemed to be filling all those periods which could not strictly be described as duty.

Then, when Jake stopped at the opposite side of the table at which she was seated, when she saw him touch Sagan's broad shoulder, this evening improbably clad in an off the shoulder confection in pale blue brocade, she felt as if she had had her face none too gently slapped. It was impossible to drag her eyes away while Sagan simpered up at Jake, apparently enjoying the masterful way he was demanding her as a partner for this dance.

'Oh, Jake,' she was saying, incredibly, 'you remembered.' Then they were on the floor and tangoing away as if their lives depended on it. And they were experts, Hana could not avoid that conclusion. Twice the size of most normal women Sagan might be, but she was nimble on her feet and moved like Margot Fonteyn while the lead guitarist, sending himself up, sang *Jealousy* with throb and passion.

There were only a few other couples dancing and they seemed to defer to the experts, hugging the edges while Sagan and Jake swooped and glided over the lecture room floor. They finished on a series of brilliant steps which took them to one corner, Sagan did a pirouette, dropped a deep curtsey, while Jake took her fingers to his lips and bowed over them. There was a burst of applause from the guests who had been wildly entertained, but it was only when the couple returned to the table that Hana realised this turn was becoming something of a tradition at the Christmas ball.

'Same time next year?' Jake smiled down at his partner as she sat down. Then without waiting for an answer he turned away. 'Thanks, Brenda.'

Brenda. That was the first time she had heard Sagan addressed by her first name. Somehow it made Hana feel excluded as nothing else could have done. Broodingly she watched the tall figure, the broad shoulders under the dark barathea, the easy swing as he walked towards the entrance. Vaguely she heard the congratulations around the table, someone accused Sagan of having been practising. 'You were even better than last year. I believe you have been meeting Jake on the sly.'

Suddenly it was more than Hana could bear, but she retained her manners to the extent of adding a laughing comment to what had already been said, then pushed back her chair with a murmur about going to the ladies' room. It was deserted in there so she had a few moments to compose herself, to lean her face against the coolness of the mirror in an effort to bring herself back to some kind of normality. Quickly, when she had got control of herself, she retouched her make-up which didn't really need it and ran a comb through her hair. A brief spray of 'Magie Noire' about her neck and shoulders and she was ready, to face the world if necessary. Only, she wondered, just how soon could one opt out of the Christmas Dance? Now it was nearly eleven and even though she had danced every dance except the tango, the time passed with exhausting slowness.

She hesitated when she reached the hall again, unwilling to rejoin the group of senior staff round the table where she had been sitting for the last half hour, she wasn't ready to be relegated to that category, not just yet. Feeling eyes on her she looked round to find James Catenby in company with quite a large party of men about his own age. They all had that prosperous, comfortable look of men who were used to having their own way, they were smoking cigars and talking so that their voices carried easily.

But James Catenby was saying nothing, he was too busy watching Hana. Although he gave no sign of recognition, she sensed a hungriness in his expression that had been missing on the previous occasions when they had met.

Trying to move casually she drifted round the room, away from the group at the door and looking with a sense of desperation for Dave, for anyone who might dance with her. The music started up again, this time something soft and smoochy. To her dismay she realised she was heading straight in the direction of Jake, now deep in conversation with Mr Castlereagh but looking at her. She veered, feeling conspicuous and irresolute, doubly so when she realised that Mrs Castlereagh was insisting her husband take her up to dance and that Jake was on his own.

From the corner of her eye a flash of silver hair told her that Mr Catenby was tracking her closely and she was prepared to do anything rather than have him touch her. She sensed that he and his party had been drinking somewhere and that he would want to hold her close in the misplaced belief that this would make him irresistible. James Catenby was just a step away from her now, she could smell the scent from his cigar. God, she thought, will he go on smoking when he's dancing?

Jake was still looking at her, a frown drawing the dark eyebrows closer together as if he was trying to decide what she was up to, then his eyes flicked momentarily from hers to the man who was so clearly in pursuit. And back to her. He took a step forward, Hana made no attempt to hide the hunted expression in her eyes and Jake smiled at her as if he had been waiting all night for such an opportunity.

'Our dance I think, Sister.' He put his arm round her waist, folded her right hand in his and as they moved away, Hana felt she was in a dream.

It was a while before he spoke but everything about their situation was so perfect, so *right*, that Hana gave herself up completely to the pleasure of it. To start with they moved harmoniously together, it was something she hadn't expected. And the mood of the music was so tranquil, so romantic, that all she could do was relax. Besides it would have been ungracious to resist the strength that was pulling her so close to him, even if she had had the inclination.

She didn't quite allow her head to droop against his shoulder but it was a close thing. Something to do with reaction after escaping from Mr Catenby. But it was also wonderfully nice to almost feel the cool touch of his skin against hers. Once or twice their faces touched, but it was so fleeting that she might have imagined it. She could smell the cologne he used, distinctive but not too obtrusive, that was one of the things she hadn't liked about Lindsay, he *had* been inclined to drench himself in the stuff.

'Was this what you wanted?' She had to pull herself back from her thoughts when he spoke to her and it was a blow to find herself looking up into eyes that were coolish, certainly a few degrees cooler than she was feeling.

'I'm sorry.' Her eyes were wide and fixed now on his mouth, a relentless line in which she saw no softness.

'I gathered,' he looked away from her as he negotiated into a comparatively clear corner, 'that you were appealing for some assistance.'

'I was.' There seemed no point in prevarication. 'Thank you.'

'That's all right.' He spoke brutally, injuring those soft feelings which just a few moments earlier had been stealing seductively over her. 'It's a pleasure.' And to underline what he had said his hand about her waist slipped marginally lower, pulled her even more firmly against him. 'In fact, I've been wanting to dance with you all evening. Only I wasn't sure that your answer wouldn't have been a polite refusal.'

'Come now, Mr Carlyon.' Damaged feelings made her speak with all the bitter sweetness she could muster, 'You must know that your word is law as far as the nurses are concerned. You just have to state what you want and we obey.'

'You,' he spoke between his teeth, 'you, Sister, are the exception to prove the rule, whatever that means. You take a delight, a perverse delight, in obstructing me in every way possible.'

'I'm sorry you should think that.' She spoke wooden-ly, wondering why all the magic had gone out of the dance, not noticing that the music had changed to something more brittle and dynamic. 'That hasn't been my intention, I assure you.'

'Don't lie to me, Sister.' As he spoke he smiled down at her, the dark eyes gleaming with an expression that wasn't amusement. 'Now, try to look as if you're en-joying yourself,' he spoke warningly and she realised that the music had stopped, that the dancers were leaving the floor, 'otherwise your boy-friend, past or present I neither know nor care, will be ready to pounce on you again.'

Catching sight of James Catenby hovering somewhere in front of them, Hana smiled up at Jake, felt his arm tighten about her as he returned a passionate glance.

'Hello Hana, Jake.' A very confident Catenby barred their way and the pair looked up from their mutual contemplation with an affectation of surprise.

'James.' Jake was as smooth as the other man on this occasion while Hana contented herself with a faint smile.

'You're looking very attractive this evening, my dear.' His gaze raked her from head to her feet in a deliberately familiar way. 'Dare I ask you for a dance?' A wave of one long hand in the direction of the band made her aware of the throb of an exotic Latin-American tune.

She shuddered slightly, unconscious of the arm tightening about her waist, pulling her with a more possessive gesture even closer. But before she could find the words to refuse him, she heard Jake's voice, deep and reassuring, just above her head saying words she could scarcely credit.

'I'm afraid you're too late, James. We've just decided to go home. Hana has a bit of a headache. It's been a bit of a din and besides we had a slightly hectic day on the wards, maybe you've heard.'

'Yes, I did hear.' James Catenby's mouth tightened in fury at being thwarted, then he seemed to make an effort to regain control, smiled and shrugged philosophically. 'Well, next time no doubt.'

'Of course.' Jake seemed to be making all her decisions for her. 'I'm sure next Christmas Hana will be pleased to keep a dance for you.' He smiled down at her. 'Ready, darling?' He scarcely waited for her dazed nod and then they were walking, in an affectionate embrace that made Angie Newcombe, hurrying across the entrance foyer, turn and gape at them.

Only when they reached the windy and ill-lit parking area did Jake Carlyon drop the loving attitude so that now his hands were hurrying her none too gently in the direction of the long red car pulled up close to the gate. Hana, shivering now, yet hardly wishing to explain that her car keys were reposing in the pocket of her coat in the cloakroom, stumbled, splashed her tights in a puddle and at last was driven to protest.

'Where on earth do you think you're taking me?'

'Home, my sweet,' he ground the words at her. 'Isn't that what we told the man in there?'

'You told the man.' She wrenched her arm from his grasp and turned to face him in the darkness. 'As far as I can recall I said nothing.'

'No,' he jeered, 'all you did was widen your big brown eyes and Sir Galahad came galloping to the rescue. If you didn't want me to take you home then you should have said.' He bent to open the door of his car. 'Get in.'

Hardly able to protest Hana allowed herself to be pushed into the passenger seat and said nothing when he pulled an anorak from the rear seat and threw it about her shoulders. She waited till he had taken the driver's seat before continuing the argument, trying to speak calmly.

'I've got my own car here. I would rather drive it home myself.'

'Well,' he shrugged as if he no longer had any interest in what she did, 'you must do what you like.'

'But,' she faltered, struck by the implacability of the profile turned against her, touched by the faint sounds of music coming to them as if from a distance, 'I left my keys inside. With my coat.'

'And what are you asking me to do?' His voice was as cold as charity, 'Are you suggesting that I go back inside, collect your coat and deliver it to you like a message boy.' He turned the key in the ignition and the car glided out of the gate. 'Forget it. This was what you wanted just a moment ago.' A flick of a switch brought some warmth stealing about her feet and legs. 'Just lie back and think of England.'

But that advice was something which Hana was incapable of taking right then. She wasn't even able to think of the inconvenience of her car and keys being left at the hospital while she was whisked off in Jake Carlyon's.

Her mind was too confused, too obsessed by the fact that she was sitting close to him, in his car, and that every nerve in her body was responding to the magic of his presence. For the first time she admitted its existence, that elusive sensation that seemed able to bind the two of them together. Was it possible that he was unaware of it?

Before she would have believed it possible they were stopping at the gate of the cottage and he came round to open the door of the car, pulling the anorak closer about her as she stepped out onto the roadside. She shivered, teeth chattering lightly as in the brilliance of the car lights she looked up at him. Then he leaned back inside and they were in darkness.

'Give me your doorkey.' He waited impatiently while she fumbled in her evening bag, feeling absurdly grateful that she had the key of the cottage with her instead of with the others as it might so easily have been. She followed him up the path, walked into the house ahead of him when he threw back the door.

She hadn't meant to make the suggestion but there was something in his expression when she turned to look at him, his face all shadowy planes in the light from the small lamp which burned on the side table.

'Would you like a cup of coffee?'

It was a moment before he answered and a glimmer in his eyes made her long to snatch back the invitation before he had the chance to accept it.

'Thanks.' Laconically he turned and closed the door behind him.

Fire raced through her veins as she stared at him, her heart was hammering against her breast, beating a deafening tattoo in her ears, warmth came and went in her cheeks.

'I'll . . .' One hand clutched at the jacket which was about to slip from her shoulders and missed. '. . . I'll just go and put the kettle on for that coffee.'

'Damn the coffee.' He took a step towards her, caught at her hands and pulled her unresisting body into his arms.

CHAPTER NINE

IT WAS a celestial trip while it lasted, his mouth persuasive, delicate at first, then becoming more forceful as he curved the softness of her body even closer to his. Hana felt her bones melt in the heat of her reactions and moaned a little when his lips left hers and he bent lower, tracing a burning path down her cheek, coming to rest in the hollow of her throat.

'You know, Hana,' his mouth was whispering against her ear now and she eased her body more comfortably to his, leaning towards that powerful hard form. 'I've fancied you since . . .' a seductive finger trailed over her skin, slipped one of the narrow straps from her smooth shoulders, paused by the long zip at the back of her dress.

Lazily her eyes opened slightly, a smile curved her mouth as she held back her head so his kiss could press into the deep hollows between her breasts. White teeth caught at her lower lip as she stifled the sounds of pleasure, arms reached about his neck, pulling his body more insistently to hers, eyes were drifting sleepily closed again when suddenly she realised he was looking at her with a long smouldering expression.

'Since . . . when?' she murmured, before his mouth stifled her question, sending any kind of rational query spinning from her mind, unable as she was to think or to plan with this insidious assault betraying her. Skilfully his lips parted hers, his mouth explored, seduced, till she knew that this time there was no stopping.

'Since . . . when?' she insisted, breathlessly, holding

her cheek against his. 'Since when?' She nibbled his ear, feeling the dark hair silkily sensuous against her cheek.

But he didn't answer, merely swept her up in his arms and began to mount the steps two at a time. She didn't even have to tell him to look out for the awkward beam at the top, it seemed he bent his head with the same instinct that led him to push open the right door at the top of the stairs.

Neither of them noticed the cat's loud protest at this abrupt intrusion, nor the way he jumped down from his chair and stalked with angry waving tail towards the door.

Jake allowed her to slide down from his arms which still imprisoned her, moulding her close to him while his lips continued their searching onslaught. She felt his fingers slide the zip so that her dress drifted from her shoulders, then his mouth was on her breast, incredibly sweet, bewildering her with the confusion of intoxicating pleasures that swept away all vestige of restraint, all she waited for was his total confession.

'Jake.' She murmured his name, smiled up at him, touched his cheeks with slender fingers. 'Tell me, since when?' For the moment she didn't see the bleakness in his eyes, the firmness about his mouth which a moment before seemed to have been promising such delight. 'You said you'd fancied me,' it was a new role for her, that of flirt and lover, but just part of the whole of being in love, 'Since when?' She longed for him to say 'Since the first moment I saw you, of course' but he didn't immediately answer, only looked down at her with that assessing gaze which made the smile slip from her mouth.

'What do you want me to say, Hana?' he asked lightly.

'The truth of course,' she lied.

'Even if you don't like it?'

'Naturally.' Her fingers were cold now and reached to pull the straps of her dress back onto her shoulders.

'Since I knew that you were . . . available.'

'Available?' The word didn't make any sense to her. Wide brown eyes stared into his. 'Available?' A glimmering of comprehension came into her mind.

'Yes.' He removed the bow tie which moments earlier he had pulled loose in a gesture of impatient frustration, thrust it into his pocket, then raked a hand through his hair. 'It's none of my business, I suppose.'

Still watching him, Hana reached for the wide stole lying at the foot of her bed, pulling it about her in a search for some modesty, waiting with deadly despair for him to continue.

'I don't know what has happened between you and Catenby, obviously you've had some kind of lovers' quarrel, hence your invitation to coffee with myself as substitute.' There was only a gentle light in the room coming from the lamp beside the bed, left on as company for Oscar, and she thought inconsequentially how drawn Jake looked. 'Only,' his lips twisted in self-derision, 'quite suddenly I found that I couldn't. I draw the line at acting as stop-gap for your lover. Especially one like James Catenby.'

Hana felt as if all the blood was draining from her heart. A sob rose in her throat but her pride would not allow her to express it so she raised her chin and faced him. Damn you, damn James Catenby and damn all men, she thought. 'Get out,' she said.

'I'm going.' One raised eyebrow mocked her, but there must be some way she could get back at him. The words were out before he could reach the door, before she had time to reflect that maybe it would be more dignified to remain silent.

'As you seem to have such a low opinion of James

Catenby I'm surprised you spend so much time with his daughter.'

He turned just before he pulled the door closed behind him. 'Now, Sister Dean, anyone would think you were jealous.' A moment later she heard the front door close followed by the roar of a powerful car engine.

It was a long time before Hana moved but at last she dragged off her lovely dress, threw herself into bed and cried till she fell asleep from sheer exhaustion.

In the morning she was bewildered but uncaring to see that her car had been delivered to the door, that the keys were lying inside the front door beside a pile of Christmas cards. It was a nightmare to think that she had to go to work but at least it was Friday, not a day when she was likely to run into Jake Carlyon. Hardly aware of what she was doing, she poured out a cup of coffee, then feeling too sick to drink it she emptied it down the sink.

The ward was only half full, most of the patients who had reached a reasonable stage in their convalescence having been discharged so they could spend Christmas at home. This was one day that Hana would have been glad to be rushed off her feet but still there was lots she could do, check on the stocks of sterile dressings and supervise the tidying of the linen cupboards. No matter what grumbles this would produce among the nurses, at this particular moment she was more concerned with her own feelings than theirs.

'What's wrong with Sister?' She heard one of the junior nurses giggling as she made up piles of towels. 'I thought after the dance she might be in a good mood.'

'Get on with that and stop wasting time.' Staff Nurse Newcombe was unusually sharp this morning too, Hana noticed with no pleasure. 'That job should be finished well before lunch time and then you can start a check on the linen that's in use in the ward.'

'That makes two of them,' the newest nurse on Fleming whispered when Angie had bustled away, quite unconscious of the fact that Hana in the still room next door could hear very clearly everything that was being said.

'Well,' her companion explained, 'Staff will be mad that she didn't get Jake to take her home.'

'What? Didn't he? Who did then?'

'I don't know,' this was said mysteriously, 'but I do know who Jake went home with.'

'Nurse,' even allowing for her unhappiness Hana's voice was severe. 'There's no gossiping allowed on Fleming Ward.' Her heels tapped angrily on the tile floor as she whirled round the corner. 'Is that understood?' She waited for an answer.

'Yes, Sister,' said the dismayed junior.

'Nurse,' Hana glowered at the girl who hadn't yet answered.

'Yes, Sister.'

'Now get on with your work.' And for all the good that will do you might as well have saved your breath, Hana thought with a fleeting shaft of amusement as she went back to her office and pulled out her notes with a weary sigh.

Suddenly the office door opened abruptly without the customary knock and he was lying against it, looking at her with a strange expression, one that she could have made no attempt to interpret even if she had been calm enough to do so.

'Mr Carlyon.' With an effort she got to her feet, turned from him and tried to give the impression that she was filing her notes into the correct alphabetical order. 'One doesn't expect to see you on a Friday.' She was surprised to hear her voice sound as normal as it did.

There was no reply and when it was impossible to play about any longer with the papers, she turned round, leaning against the drawer of the filing cabinet so that it glided back into position.

His expression narrowed a shade and he took a step towards her, one hand reached out towards her, but she moved so that his hand fell on her blue uniformed arm instead of bare skin. She knew that she could not stand such an intimacy. Not after last night. She turned so that his hand fell away, went to her desk and sat at it, refusing to look up at him. 'What can I do for you, Mr Carlyon?' Her coolness was in total contradiction to the wild tattoo of her pulses. Brown eyes flicked up towards his, then down. She picked up a pen, drew a sheet of blank paper towards her and frowned.

'I've come, Hana, to apologise for last night. I don't usually behave like that. Not even when I'm trying to save a girl from a James Catenby.' An unexpected spark of humour lit his voice, stilled the hand writing incomprehensibles on the paper, caused a flicker of pleasure deep down in the base of her stomach.

'As I say, I don't usually behave like that.'

Hana remembered she was in no mood this morning for humour, her voice crackled with as much starch as her apron as she rose, sweeping him with a dismissive glance. 'You surprise me.' She was pleased when she saw the faint smile fade from his lips, tried to forget how those lips had felt about hers last night. She couldn't quite decide if he sighed, for he spoke again almost at once.

'Well, I've done what I came to do. I'm sorry if I said things that offended you. I have no right to comment on your private life.'

'I'm glad you realise that,' she said smoothly as she sat

down again. 'But you shouldn't have troubled to come in specially this morning. I don't consider my feelings are all that important.' Which was a lie. 'Oh, and,' she frowned over some scribbles, 'thank you for having my car delivered.'

'Think nothing of it, Sister.' Sardonically he turned finally to the door and a moment later she was watching the tall figure, dressed with his usual blend of elegance and informality, stride away from her, she saw his dark head disappear at the bend of the corridor and was left with an aching emptiness. Just then she caught sight of the junior nurse, the one she had been reprimanding before Jake arrived, only now she was looking with pop-eyed interest through the glass door of the office, presumably having enjoyed a ring-side seat at the performance.

Hana pushed back her chair in a mood to tick the girl off severely, then all the fire seemed to ebb away from her and she slumped back onto her seat and watched without a trace of satisfaction as the child scuttled away with a look of abject terror on her face. It might have been funny if Hana had felt the least bit like laughing.

But she didn't. She felt like weeping and that was impossible. So instead, she leaned her head in one hand, felt her skin burning with fever and began to sneeze. Icicles trickled down her backbone and she knew with a feeling of sheer relief that she was incubating 'flu germs.

It was bliss to be ordered a complete rest by the house physician.

'Go to bed, Hana, and keep warm.' Dr Atkinson, a local GP who was doctor for the hospital staff, smiled as he issued the instructions and scribbled a prescription. 'Will you have anyone to look after you at home? You could always get a bed in one of the side wards if you want, you'd have someone to look after you and bring you some food.'

'Oh, no thanks.' She tried a joke, 'I always think hospital is the last place I want to be when I'm sick. You never get any peace. No,' she said, and sneezed, 'right now my idea of heaven is my own bed with the curtains pulled, a hot water bottle and the 'phone off the hook.'

'All right.' He wasn't entirely convinced. 'But I don't like to think of you being on your own with no-one to make as much as a cup of tea. Would you like me to get Pat to come in and do something.' Pat was his wife, a staff-nurse on one of the other wards.

'No, really, I'll be fine. There's masses of tinned food in the house and I shall be able to totter up to the bathroom and heat some soup. I promise you I shan't starve. Besides I could do to lose some weight.'

'You girls and weight problems.' His eyes drifted approvingly over her figure. 'I can never understand them.'

'It's all right for you,' Hana protested as she rose and picked up the prescription. 'Thin as a lath, you'll never gain an extra pound. Anyway thanks, Stan, I'll be all right by the middle of the week so I'll probably be back on duty by Wednesday.'

But Hana was being too optimistic for she was unable to get out of bed till the following Wednesday and even then she felt weak and depressed, in spite of the tonic which Stan Atkinson brought when he came on a visit. Friends had brought supplies of foil-covered plates which required only to be popped into the oven for a short while and several puddings of the invalid food variety which were supposed to tempt her appetite.

By the Thursday she was feeling much better physically and on Friday was well enough to enjoy Mary's visit in the afternoon, a fact which her friend's professional eye soon discovered as she bustled about the kitchen preparing tea.

'Well, I'm glad to see you looking so much better, love. Teapot in here, did you say?'

Hana, who had been pushed into the kitchen chair, could hardly help laughing. 'I'm quite capable of making us a cup of tea, you know. It's 'flu I had, not galloping consumption.'

'Mmm.' Mary stood with her hand on the sinktop waiting for the kettle to boil. 'You were looking pretty bad when I popped in the other day.'

'You hardly had the chance to see me,' Hana protested. 'And if I had had any idea you were meaning to come I would have locked the door. I should hate if I had passed the virus on to you. In fact, I should be waiting on you, not the other way round.'

'Nonsense, I'm as strong as a horse.' Mary grinned and passed a satisfied hand over her bulge before she poured boiling water over the tea, then put the pot under its warm cosy on the tray. 'Come on then, into the other room now and we'll sit at the fire.'

'How's Nicky?' Hana sipped her tea and thought how nice it was to have Mary to talk to.

'Dying to see you again. Since that day you took him to the beach he's been pestering us about it. In fact he's on edge in case you and I go off there on our own this afternoon. I had to bribe him to stay with Ted's mother.'

'Well, I enjoyed that day as much as he did.' Her mind drifted back to a Sunday in late autumn, a day of glorious sunshine when she had offered to act as baby-sitter when Ted and Mary went to visit elderly relatives. It had been such a perfect calming day that Hana had promised to take him again sometime. 'Tell him,' she said on impulse, 'that we'll go again some time over the holidays. Just for a quick walk and then he can come back here for tea.'

'Oh that would be marvellous, Hana. And in fact it

saves me asking you if you would have him the Sunday after Christmas. If you're not doing anything that is.' She looked anxiously at her friend's face. 'But maybe you won't be feeling up to that?'

'Of course I will. Are you and Ted going away for the day?'

'We've half-promised to take Ted's mother to visit her sister in Bideford. It's a long wearying trip for him and he's not the world's best traveller. Or visitor,' she added with rueful truth. She took Hana's cup and refilled it. 'See me,' she grinned, 'taking over your house for you. 'Yes, it's funny about Nicky, you're one of the few people he really wants to come and see.'

'Flattery will get you everywhere. Now you've got a baby-sitter for life.'

'That brings me to something else. We would love you to have Christmas lunch with us, Hana. There will just be four of us, Ted's Mum and Nicky so you'd be doing us a favour if you would come.'

But Hana had refused too many invitations not to have her excuses pat and ready. And she was still too bruised, not only by what had happened with Lindsay but much more by the scene she had had with Jake Carlyon. Her confidence had taken a terrible knock, even now she wasn't ready to believe that people really *wanted* her company. Christmas was for families, her family was far away and she had no intention of thrusting herself on other people.

'That's kind of you, Mary, but it's still what I told you when you mentioned it before. I'm expecting a friend for lunch on Christmas day. She'd be on her own as well,' each time she told the lie it seemed to gain more credibility, 'and I'm looking forward to seeing her. We haven't met since we were training together.'

'Oh.' Mary hesitated, taking no trouble to conceal her

doubts, 'I see. Well,' she brightened, 'why don't you bring her along as well? The more the merrier.'

'Thanks, love, but I'd better not. She's expecting just to have lunch with me, I don't know how she would react to a group of strangers.' Her friend, decided Hana, was beginning to sound more and more unlikely, a neurotic freak in fact, but she was surprised when Mary put an altogether different interpretation on the matter.

'Hana . . .' she smiled almost coyly, 'I'm beginning to have doubts about this friend of yours.'

'What on earth do you mean?' In spite of all her endeavours Hana could not restrain the faint warmth in her cheeks.

'I mean, no matter how much you keep talking about "she", your friend is beginning to sound more and more like a "he".'

Suffused with relief Hana actually smiled. This was something she could deny with total certainty. She was so disillusioned with the opposite sex that she was unlikely to *invent* another one. No, she had a very firm idea of what her friend looked like and she wasn't the least bit masculine, in fact she was a man-hater just like herself. 'No, I'm sorry to disappoint you.'

'Oh?' Mary, still uncertain whether or not she was hearing the truth studied her friend intently. 'Well, I can't see why you should find it so unlikely.' There was a thoughtful pause. 'By the way, you haven't told me anything about the dance.'

'The dance. Oh the hospital dance,' she said as if she had been to twenty. 'It was very good. You know what a hospital dance is like, Mary. Oh and the decorations were out of this world,' she exaggerated. 'A great effort.'

'It wasn't the decorations I was asking about.'

'No?' Suddenly Hana felt strong enough to get up and

remove the tray. 'Well, as I said, it was like all the hospital dances you've ever been to. I enjoyed it.' She began rinsing cups under the hot tap while Mary picked up a tea towel.

'What I want to know is who danced with who. And especially who danced with you.'

'Oh, I think I did the rounds,' Hana spoke complacently. 'It was all very proper.'

'And Jake?' Mary transferred her attention from the cup she was polishing to Hana's profile. 'Did he dance with you.'

'Like I said, everyone danced with everyone else. Actually his tango with Sister Sagan was the *tour de force* of the evening.'

'Oh, that,' Mary laughed. 'They both love to show off.'

'Mmm. Jake maybe. And yes,' she appeared to consider. 'Sagan too is a bit extrovert.'

'I wouldn't call Jake an extrovert, actually.' She paused to lift the cups and saucers over to the cupboard. 'What about Tanya? Was she there?'

'No.'

'Mmm. I thought she would have been. With father if not with Jake.'

'Well,' Hana spoke with misleading calm, 'she was with neither. In fact,' she swished a hot soapy cloth round the sink, 'I'm wondering if Angie Newcombe has displaced Tanya. He *was* dancing with her rather more than the calls of duty demanded.'

'Oh.' It was impossible for Mary to keep the disappointment from her voice. 'Can't men be absolute *fools* sometime? Even sensible men like Jake Carlyon.'

Hana frowned, pretending that she had no idea what her friend was talking about, and diverted the conversation from that particular path. But before she finally went Mary returned again to the matter of Christmas day.

'Well, Hana, if I can't persuade you to come to us for lunch, maybe you'll come and have a drink in the evening.'

'Oh,' Hana said cagily, 'will there be anyone else there?'

'No.' Mary's tone indicated that she knew only too well what Hana was thinking. 'No, it will just be two of us. Three if Ted's mother hasn't gone home by then. Oh, and bring your friend with you if she's still here. Did you say she was staying the night with you?'

'No, I didn't say that. In fact I'm sure she'll be gone by then. And a visit to you and Ted will just round the day off nicely. I won't leave it too late for I'd like to see Nicky and hear about what Father Christmas has brought.'

And in fact Hana found that Christmas spent alone wasn't the dreary affair she might have imagined. It was a particularly mild day with a little weak sunshine so she spent half an hour sitting on a chair in a sheltered corner of the garden while the pheasant she had bought wafted deliciously towards her through the open kitchen window.

She treated herself to prawn avocado for her first course, the pheasant washed down with a quarter bottle of sparkling wine and home-made mincemeat tart with a generous quantity of whipped cream. When she had eaten, carved off a few choice pieces of the bird for Oscar and washed up, she took a cup of coffee back to the sitting room, meaning to switch on the television. But instead, overcome by the unusually rich meal and the wine, she felt herself drifting off into sleep.

When the time arrived for the reluctantly promised visit to Mary she was glad to leave the house, to escape for a few hours from the solitude where her inclination to look back regretfully could be pushed aside for only so long. Seeing Jake again yesterday, even so briefly, had brought back all the pain, the anguish which she had been trying to pretend didn't exist.

The Christmas Eve carol singing round the wards was something she had always loved, but never until now had it held so much personal suffering. She had heard them approaching the ward in the late afternoon, gave a signal to Nurse Chalmers to switch off the lights and waited with the same excitement, the same nostalgic wistfulness as the others for the singers to turn the corner and come into the ward.

At first she hadn't realised he was there, but something pulled her eyes to the taller figures at the back of the group, where the light from the hand-held old-fashioned lanterns didn't quite reach and her heart gave a great leap. It was impossible to say whether it had been his gaze that had drawn her attention, foolish even to allow her thoughts to play with such an idea, but there was a distinct frisson which told her it was at least a possibility.

Even Angie Newcombe's presence by her side could not stop her eyes seeking his face again and again and she fancied it was his voice, strong and melodious, which filled out the deeper notes as they joined in the age-old words. But all too soon it was over, as the choir began to sing 'Once in Royal David's City' the choristers turned and made their way from Fleming Ward, their singing fading and disappearing in the distance. King's College Choir it may not have been, but it was singularly moving nonetheless and Hana had to brush away a tear as she gave permission to turn the lights back on.

But that glimpse of him, brief and unsatisfactory though it might have been was enough to bring all the frustrated longings surging, like a renewal of the fever back into her blood. And she admitted to herself as she had a dozen despairing times when she lay in bed, that what she had once thought a broken heart was nothing of the kind. Lindsay had bruised her pride, humbled her in front of her friends, but her heart had emerged unscathed.

Now she really knew what it meant to say your heart was broken. If she put her hand where she knew hers to be, she could feel a definite, a vague but definite ache. Something told her it was a pain that would be very hard to shift.

It was a relief that she had only one empty day mid-week to fill for on Boxing Day she was back on the ward while Staff Nurse Newcombe took her holiday. Then Friday to be got through and the weekend and her promised outing with Nicky on the Sunday.

In spite of her early arrival, just a few minutes before ten o'clock, Nicky was impatiently watching for her through the window, had thrown open the door and was scampering down the steps before she had finally stopped the car.

'I'm glad it's a nice day, Hana.' He pulled her into the kitchen where his parents were just tidying away the remains of their breakfast. 'Otherwise we might not have been able to go to the beach.'

'Well, I don't know,' when she had greeted Ted and Mary, Hana peered out of the window, 'although it's dry it's not all that sunny. I'm wondering if this is a day for the beach after all.'

'Oh . . .' Nicky began to protest.

'Quiet, Nick,' his father ordered. 'Now, when you're with Hana she'll decide what you're going to do. If she doesn't want to go to the beach that's that. Now, come with me and we'll collect all your things so you'll be prepared for everything that comes.'

'Well, what do you think?' When the two had gone from the kitchen Hana turned to her friend.

'It depends on you, love. Don't let him drag you to the beach if it's too cold for you. Remember you're just getting over 'flu.'

'Oh it's not too cold for me.' Hana laughed. 'I'm used to picnics in all kinds of weather conditions. Dad used to take us all away from our favourite TV programmes when we were young to go out exploring and I'm sure it did us good. Besides, I'm well over the 'flu by now, I feel fit as a fiddle. No, it was Nicky I was thinking about. Are you sure it isn't too cold for him?'

'No. It'll do him good. He'll have his warm trews and his anorak and I'll put in his wellies so you needn't worry about him getting his feet wet. For I know him, no matter what you say he won't be able to resist looking at those pools in the rocks. He'll be so disappointed if you don't go, Hana, although I told him you might not want to.'

'That's settled then.' Hana got up as Nick came back into the kitchen with his father. 'We'll go back to the cottage and have some cocoa and biscuits, then we'll heat some soup and put it in a flask, butter some rolls and we'll have our lunch on the beach. We won't wait too long,' she warned. 'After all, it is the end of December. Then,' she said, 'when we've had enough we'll go back to the cottage, pile some logs on the fire and I'll make hamburgers, beans and chips. How does that suit you?'

'Super,' said Nick with flattering ecstasy.

And the day went rather well. Nick, probably having been warned by his father, was on his best behaviour and tried to control his itching impatience to be on the beach.

But at last they arrived at a small cove where they had been once or twice before during the late summer and settled themselves and their possessions in a little sheltered bay. It was convenient that the car could be pulled almost on to the sand so little carrying was involved. It was simply a case of opening the car doors, lifting out the box with their picnic things and spreading a tartan rug on the sand.

They spent a pleasant hour walking back and forward along the soft dry sand where the tide rarely reached, searching for pretty shells which were collected in a plastic bag specially brought for the purpose. Then they sat on the rug for a bit spotting seabirds which Hana tried to identify from her bird book. They watched some oyster-catchers dabbling about in the tide as it lapped back and forth over the rocks and sand, then lay back on the rug to stare at the gulls as they wheeled overhead before dropping down onto a cliffside a little way down the coast.

As they ate their soup, dipping their buttery rolls into the steaming cups before biting, a faint sun glimmered hazily overhead, encouraging Nicky to pull down the zip of his anorak.

'It's hot,' he protested as if they were suffering from unexpectedly soaring temperatures.

'Yes, but the soup's hotter than the sun,' Hana said, and was unutterably pleased when he giggled and spluttered into his soup.

But the sun, veiled as it might be by the drift of light cloud, could hardly be denied and when they had finished eating and the box was safely stowed away in the car it was impossible to keep Nicky from his favourite occupation of crouching down on the rocks beside some of the pools left by the tide and watching the busyness of the insect life.

'Here, Hana,' he whispered imperatively and she joined him, sharing his fascination with all that was happening below the surface.

'See that one there, Hana.' He pointed to a minute piece of wriggling thread, 'It's just eaten one of those. Those, do you see.' And to his delight another of the scarcely visible cells disappeared to reappear like a tiny embryo inside the almost transparent fish. 'Maybe it'll turn it into a baby,' he said chattily. Then when he received no answer. 'That's where the babies come from, you know.'

'Yes, I know.'

'Only,' an uncertainty overcame him, 'I didn't know you had to eat them first.' But before he could invite Hana to comment on his theory he gave a subdued cry of excitement as a tiny crab scuttled from one stone to another.

It was too much to expect him to resist putting his hands in the water but he soon realised how cold it was and shook his fingers, putting them under his arms for comfort.

'Had enough?' Hana asked and sighed, but only a little, when he shook his head. 'Well, keep your hands out of the water or you'll get really cold and then we will have to go home. Now if you'll be very careful I'll go back to the car and get a towel to dry your hands properly. See,' she turned back his cuffs, 'you've got your anorak wet as well.' And she tutted in mock irritation but Nicky only grinned mischievously. 'Don't fall in or it'll be over your boots,' she admonished as she left to walk the few yards up the deserted beach to their picnic spot.

She hadn't gone more than a couple of steps when she heard him call out to her.

'Oh, Hana.' It was a nervous little cry. 'I couldn't help

it. I slipped on the sea-weed.'

'Oh, Nicky,' she sounded a little bit vexed. 'I hope you haven't got your feet wet.'

'No,' he said hopefully as she reached his side. 'No, the water hasn't come over.'

'Come on then,' she said bracingly, holding out her hand, 'pull your foot out. Don't stand there like Hop-Along Cassidy.'

'My foot.' Nicky bit his lower lip and frowned in concentration. 'My foot, won't . . . come . . . Hana.'

'Of course it will.' Hana laughed and dropped onto her knees, grateful that she was wearing an old pair of ski pants which gave her protection from the rocks. 'Come on, I'll help you.' She took hold of the top of the wellington. 'Now,' she joked, 'All together, 'pu . . . ull.'

'It won't come. Oh, Hana.' His mouth trembled. 'It's stuck.'

'Of course it will.' She forced her suddenly stiff lips into a smile, hoping it looked more genuine than it felt. 'And if it won't, then we'll just have to pull your foot out of your wellington and forget about it. Your wellie not your foot,' her voice quavered, but she didn't think Nicky had noticed.

But ten minutes later she had to confess that the foot was as firmly wedged in the rock's crevice as the wellington. More so. She fought to retain her calm in a situation suddenly filled with menace, tried to force herself to think calmly.

'I'm just going up to the Mini to get a car jack, darling. I'm sure I'll be able to lever the rock away from your foot. Then you'll be able to pull it out.'

A moment later, having despairingly noticed that there wasn't a living soul in sight, she came running back, the jack in her hand, wishing it wasn't such a puny little thing with which to try to lever away what seemed to be a ton of immovable rock. Then she saw something which she prayed Nicky hadn't noticed. The water which had been as high as his ankles was now half-way up the calf. And that meant, she cast a desperate look round about her to confirm her fears, the tide was coming in.

For several panic-stricken minutes she wrested with the useless car jack, then put it down. She pressed her fingers to her teeth, hardly realising that her hands were streaked with blood from the sharp edges of the tool.

'Now, Nick.' She smiled down at him. 'I'm going to have to get help. I want you to be a good boy till I get back. Don't struggle. That will only make your foot more swollen.' She pointed in the direction of a roof she could see at the top of a road, a different one from the one they had come by. 'I'll ask if I can use their telephone and I'll come right back. Now, you'll be all right. See, I'll fold up the rug so that you have a comfortable place to sit.' She watched his struggle to get his bottom onto the rug, not daring to say anything that might make him realise the frightened danger of his position. But the fear was there in the eyes he turned up to her.

'If you can't find a man, Hana,' his mouth trembled, 'will you come back yourself.'

'Of course.' She smiled, hugged him and stood up. 'Keep watching the car, darling.' She pointed a hand in the direction of the road which climbed away from the beach, 'when I get to the top I'll honk and you must wave.'

He heart was hammering with anxiety as she drove the car at breakneck speed up the twisting road, remembered to sound the horn at the bend which took her out of sight, spared a second for a brief downward glance and thought she saw a faint wave. Sobs tore from her throat but she gained control of herself as the roof she had glimpsed from the beach was translated into a small bungalow.

Brakes shrieked as she threw herself from the car, raced up the path and hammered at the door. Please, please, she closed her eyes and prayed but there was no sound coming from the interior. She ran to the window, pressed her face against the grimy glass and saw that the house was empty. The only thing that might have gladdened her heart was a telephone, she would have been prepared to break into the house to use it but there was none, and no sign of wires as she ran back to where she had left her car.

She drove like a mad thing along the narrow road, praying that she would meet no oncoming traffic, then to her relief she saw another roof, this time a much larger one nestling in the folds of countryside and from the chimneys of which a thin plume of smoke was rising.

Only vaguely did she realise that chance had brought her to the one door in all the district which she knew. She had been here twice before, the fact registered without her understanding properly.

'Jake, Jake.' Tears came as she hammered on the door, then she wrenched the large highly polished brass bell-pull, heard it clanging distantly, but without waiting any longer she turned the door knob and pushed the heavy wood door back. She stood in the centre of the hall calling his name.

Then a door on the upper floor opened, she heard his footsteps on the stairs but her eyes were too blurred to see him.

'Oh God, Jake,' she held her hands out, 'help me.'

'Hana,' Strong arms folded round her. 'Sh . . . Sh.' She felt his mouth against her hair, her sobbing was stilled. 'My darling. Hush.'

'Help me, Jake.' Don't let me faint she prayed. Please God. Please!

Firm hands moved to her shoulders, shook her just a little. 'Tell me, Hana,' he said grimly.

CHAPTER TEN

'Go AND dial 999, Hana.' His appearance of grim purpose restored some of her calm. 'Get the fire brigade, tell them what's happened. It's at Powham beach. I'll get a crowbar and some ropes and bring the car round to the front door. I've got everything else I might need in the car.' Fortunately she was so busy dialling the numbers that the significance of that hardly penetrated her brain.

Half a minute later they were driving out of the gates, then roaring up the hill and along the narrow lanes leading to the bay. Hana sat forward on the edge of her seat, trying to control her agitation and wondering vaguely why she hadn't known they were so close to Clyston. It had never occurred to her that Dene House was within two miles of the bay.

Neither of them spoke, but once Jake reached out his hand, clasped hers briefly, comfortingly, for a few minutes, then gave all his attention to throwing the large car round the tight bends. When they reached the top where the land dropped so suddenly away towards the sea, Hana, searching for the tiny figure, saw nothing moving and moaned, pressing her knuckles against her mouth.

'Please, sound the horn, Jake.' And he did, he kept sounding it as the car raced down the spiralling track and at last drew up fiercely on the edge of the beach. The door of the Jaguar was opened before it came to a stop and Hana was flying across the sand to where Nicky was trapped. The sea didn't seem to have advanced a great deal but . . . she wondered with increasing panic, where,

where was he? At last her eyes focused clearly, she saw the bundle on the rocks and then dropped down thankfully beside him, not even aware of the coldness of the water.

'It's all right, Nicky.' Now that she was back in the position of responsibility she was able to pretend a calm she wasn't feeling and she smiled reassuringly, noticing his tear-streaked face and the way he was bravely trying to respond.

'The water's in my boot now, Hana.' He wrinkled his face as if he might cry again. 'It's all squelchy.'

'Never mind.' She put an arm about him. 'It'll soon be over. I've brought Jake with me.' She half-turned as Jake, carrying the crowbar as well as his medical bag, which he dropped on the dry sand, came clambering over the rocks towards them.

'Uncle Jake!'

'Hi, Nick.' The greeting was uttered in a matter-of-fact voice that did much for the morale of the other two. Then he dropped to his knees beside Hana, as oblivious as she of the sea water lapping over the rocks and soaking his clothes. 'This is a fine pickle to get into.' As he spoke and smiled at the child his hands were exploring the deep narrow crevice into which the foot was locked. 'But never mind, I think we'll manage to get you out. And guess what,' he grinned mischievously, 'if I can't manage it on my own, then Hana's asked the fire brigade to come and help.'

'The fire brigade.' Nick didn't seem certain that this was such a good idea and he drew a sobbing breath while he considered.

'Now,' Jake got the crowbar and tested it against the rock on either side of the gap. Hana looking up at him, seeing the dark hair blowing in the increasingly boisterous wind, the serious way his eyebrows were drawn together as he concentrated on the best approach to the task, felt herself swamped by a wave of longing for him. Something had happened back there at Dene House, something which had altered her life completely. Only she couldn't remember what it was.

Suddenly he glanced towards them and caught the expression on her face, and there was a brief answering flash in his eyes before he turned his attention to Nicky, explaining to him exactly as he did to his patients in hospital what he was going to do.

'Now I'm going to try to move this stone, old son, you can see that can't you?'

'Yes.'

'And your foot, is it cold?'

'It's freezing. Oh, I'm all freezing, Uncle Jake.' And he shivered.

'Well, it's a good thing your foot's cold for that's a help. Now,' he looked at the woman who had her arms about him, 'you hang on to Hana and if anything hurts, then just yell.' He smiled as if it was all part of a game. 'But all the time you must keep trying to pull out your foot, do you understand, Nick?'

'Yes.'

'Right, here we go.'

Holding Nick's head close to her, Hana kept her eyes on Jake, saw that he was levering all the weight of his powerful frame on the strong crowbar, that the veins were standing out on his forehead with the exertion.

'Pull,' she commanded Nick, and added her own efforts by grasping the wet top of his wellington and trying to assist the process. But there was no change, the foot seemed as immovably lodged as it had been before. Several times more Jake tried to lever the rocks sufficiently, but all his efforts seemed to have not the slightest result.

He made a sign to Hana and they withdrew to the beach.

'I'm going to give him an injection, knock him out, can you prepare a syringe, Hana? We might have a better chance if we can slice off the boot. After all,' he frowned, 'the foot must have got in there, it ought to be able to get out. But I don't want him to be struggling if I happen to catch him while I'm trying to cut him out.' He glanced up towards the top of the cliff, 'Where the hell is the fire brigade?'

Silently Hana set about fixing the needle on the phial of anaesthetic and stood ready with it until Jake nodded briefly at her to signify that he had found the necessary scalpels for slicing through the thick plastic.

'Right, Hana, if you'll give it to him . . .' In spite of the horror of the circumstances she felt a tiny thrill of satisfaction that they were involved in something together, something where trust was as crucial as in the struggle for life. She turned towards Nicky and the injection was administered almost before he knew what had happened.

'That's just a tiny jab so you won't feel anything when Jake is getting your foot out.' But before she had finished talking his eyelids were beginning to droop with the effects of the powerful drug.

Things then began to move into top gear. Hana rolled the blanket and placed it where Nicky's head could be supported well clear of the water and, following Jake's example, she lay down on the rocks, supporting the knee of the trapped leg while he with a few swift sure strokes sliced away the upper part of the wellington. Then it became more difficult, when the progress was completely blind and had to depend entirely on the surgeon's sensitive fingers following the outline of the boot, cutting with the razor sharp knife so that the delicate flesh underneath should not be injured. And all the time the water was lapping higher, splashing over his face as he worked feverishly.

'The boot . . . should come off now.' He paused to get his breath back after his exertions. 'I've cut right down the centre front and if only I could reach the heel, I might be able to pull it off backwards, only . . . the gap narrows there and I doubt if I can get my hand in.' He frowned, 'If I could find a strong stick I might . . .'

'Let me try.' Hana jumped up, pulled off her drenched anorak and pushed back the sleeve of her pullover. 'My hand is a bit smaller than yours.'

'I think you'll find it too much to move. It's wedged solid and it'll take a fair bit of strength but . . . have a go. Anyway,' as he moved over to allow her more access he looked up towards the top of the rise, 'the fire brigade is here. We'll have a last chance at getting him out when they come and then . . .'

Fortunately Hana was too involved in her efforts to feel the thrill of terror that his words would normally have caused. She was lying face down in six inches of restless water, her fingers following the slender lines of the calf till they encountered the hacked-off top of the wellington. She gasped as the water washed over her face and nose, then went on with her probing, trying to ease the plastic away from the heel so that her fingers could get a firm grasp.

It was impossible, for the accident had compressed the boot at the rear of the foot and the weight of the child was adding to the problem.

'If you could lift him just a bit,' she gasped to Jake, who was dividing his attention between her effort and the rapid approach of the fire waggon, and then when the body of the child was eased a little she was able to hook one finger into the back of the heel. 'Got it.' Her heart lifted as she felt the boot move a little and she exerted all her strength till she thought her finger would break.

Somewhere in the distance she heard a flurry of activity, heard Jake shout something about levers, but she was too engrossed in the slight movement, a sliding, as she exerted all the pressure of which she was capable on the wellington. 'It's coming.' Her heart was pumping fiercely so she paused, lowered her face onto her upper arm for a second to regain her strength.

But it was Jake's softly spoken, 'Good girl,' that gave her the determination to continue, even though she had already exerted every ounce of energy she possessed.

In the end the boot came away quite suddenly, as if there had been a slackening of the pressure, and it was an intense disappointment when the foot, now bare of sock or boot, didn't slide out quite easily. But now that there were several men all armed with various levers and crowbars to add their weight to Jake's, the rocks were forced to relinquish their victim.

Totally exhausted, Hana was content to hold Nicky close to her, to kiss his cheek with a kind of desperate relief as the men prepared for a tremendous effort to force the rocks apart. To one side, two of the firemen, sledge hammers at the ready in case they had to smash the rocks, stood waiting but fortunately they were not required.

When the men heaved in unison Hana was able to pull out the foot, not with ease but with a little manipulation while the aperture was increased by a fraction of an inch. For a moment she sat back on her heels, her mouth pressed to Nicky's face with a prayer of thankfulness in her heart, then the tears came flooding down her cheeks and she stumbled with his weight while willing hands reached out to help her down from the rocks.

Jake took Nicky from her and strode across the sand to the Jaguar, wrapped Nicky in one of the blankets from the rear seat and draped another about Hana's sodden figure. Then she was settled into the passenger seat, Nicky was placed in her arms and the door was slammed. Shivering now, she watched Jake go back and have a word with the firemen, pick up his things as well as her soaked anorak from the sand. Then she saw him go to her car and return holding out her handbag.

'Give me your keys, Hana. One of the men says he'll run it back to the cottage for you.'

Stiff hands fumbled in the outer pocket and handed over the keys.

'You're making a habit of going home without your car.' He grinned, defeating the fatigue and cold etched so clearly in his features. 'You'll do that once too often.'

Seconds later they were driving up the hill, down which they had hurtled just a few minutes earlier, although it felt like years. It seemed blissful to be out of the cold and with a faint warmth circulating about them. Then they were at Dene House and Hana found herself following Jake who was carrying Nicky up the wide front steps and into the hall.

There she discovered she was being ordered about with the same bossiness which senior consultants were in the habit of demonstrating when they were in the wards. Only at this moment she didn't mind in the least being told what to do.

'You go on up, Hana, and get a bath organised for yourself. There's plenty of hot water so take as much as you like. You must be chilled to the bone.'

'But Nicky, I'll have . . .' But it was a half-hearted protest.

'I'll look after Nicky. I won't bath him but I'll take his

wet things off and put him to bed with some hot water bottles.'

'His foot's badly bruised.' While they had been in the car she had seen the dark contusions all along the bone at the side of his foot.

'Yes, it'll be painful for a day or two, but my main concern at the moment is to see that neither you nor he develop pneumonia.' Something about his expression was so tender and . . . and . . . tender that she felt a blush starting at the soles of her feet and working its way up. Then the realisation of how she must look, hair and clothes drenched with sea water, face blue with cold and now red with embarrassment, made her turn away.

'You'll want some dry things to put on.' Still carrying the boy he walked with her up the stair. 'Go in here,' he pushed open a door, 'this is my mother's bedroom. She keeps a supply of everything here so take what you want. I know there's a warm dressing-gown, that will fit you even if her other things won't. Now, off you go and have that bath.'

'What about you.' Hana paused with her fingers on the bathroom door, 'You don't want to get chilled either.'

Jake paused, a faint smile on his face, eyebrows raised in the mocking position so usual that Hana wondered why her heart was beating in wild agitation. One would almost think . . .

'Is that an invitation, Sister Dean?'

For a moment she couldn't think what he meant and almost at once he went on as he turned away with Nicky. 'Don't worry, I'll have a shower while you're in the bath so there's no need to hurry.'

And it was only when Hana was in the bathroom, watching the satisfying gush of steaming water into the

deep tub that she wondered if he could have possibly
meant *that*.

It was some time later that Hana, feeling ridiculously
self-conscious, ventured out of the bedroom onto the
deep carpet of the landing. All was perfectly still, just as
she imagined Dene House always was late on a Sunday
afternoon in mid-winter. Only today hadn't been exactly
a normal Sunday. Taking her courage in both hands, she
picked up the skirt of the long fluffy dressing-gown, a
luxurious garment in some kind of mohair with a zip
reaching from neck to hem, and walked downstairs.

When she reached the hall faint sounds of dishes being
rattled took her feet in the direction of the kitchen and
when she pushed open the door she found Jake there,
hair still damp from his shower, standing waiting for a
kettle to boil. Dark eyes flicked up and saw her in the
doorway, studied her with that intensity which had been
so familiar at their first meeting. Hana had a vague
impression of a modern kitchen, oven built into the
units, ceramic hob, but with a lot of wood that suited the
age and character of the house, cork tiles on the floor
with here and there an old-fashioned peg rug to add a bit
of colour. But all these things were to be noted in detail
and approved later. Now she was too conscious of this
emotion existing between them, this feeling that even
now was making blood surge in her veins simply because
they were looking at each other. Only his words were
banal enough and he turned as the kettle boiled to pour
it into the teapot.

'You found everything you wanted?'

'Yes, thank you.' There was the merest quaver in her
voice which she tried to disguise with a faint laugh. 'But
I'm afraid you were right. Your mother's other clothes

were too small, but I'll be able to make do with this and her slippers. And I used her hair drier.' She paused. 'How's Nick?'

'He's still asleep, although the anaesthetic should have worn off, but the sleep will do him no harm. I wondered if you might have liked to go to bed. You must have suffered as much shock as he did.'

'Yes.' The thought of the accident returned to make her feel sick with the horror of it. 'Oh, Jake,' fiercely she bit her lip, 'if you hadn't been at home . . . I can't forgive myself. If anything had . . .'

'Hana,' a few strides brought him to her side, he put his hands on her shoulders and gazed down at her. 'Don't say that. It was an accident, something none of us could have foreseen. If you hadn't found the courage to do what you did, then things really could have been much worse.'

'I can't imagine,' her frail self-control broke and she sobbed, 'what Mary and Ted are going to say. They *trusted* me and I let them down.'

'Hush.' It was almost worth the anguish of her thoughts and fears to find herself folded in his arms, to be able to lay her face on his chest and allow her misery to wash over her for a few seconds. 'I've telephoned them and they know what happened.'

'Wh . . . what? How did you know where to contact them?'

'I've met Ted's aunt and remembered her name and thought it best to ring and let them know what had happened. They're coming here to pick Nick up but they won't arrive till about seven.'

'Were they very angry?'

'Of course they weren't angry. If they had been *I* would have felt very angry with them. Now, be a good girl,' surprisingly she felt the pressure of his mouth against her hair, 'don't soak my shirt or I'll have to go and change again.'

Hana giggled and allowed herself to be led towards the morning room where two huge leather armchairs were pulled up close to a crackling log fire. Quietly content, she watched while he poured two cups of tea, then spiked some scones on a long brass toasting fork, accepting them for buttering when he handed them to her. They had several cups of tea and cake as well as the scones before he sat back, with a sigh of satisfaction, crossed legs stretched out towards the blaze, looking at her with that strange expression which made the colour come and go in her cheeks.

'You know,' there was a teasing note in his voice which she had heard often enough when he spoke to other people, seldom to her, 'this is my idea of a perfect Sunday afternoon. If it wasn't for one or two minor points.'

'Yes.' She smiled, wrenching her eyes from his and gazing into the crackling flames, 'I'm sorry.'

'Sorry?' He crooked that tantalising eyebrow, even without looking at him she knew the expression he wore.

'Sorry,' she shrugged, 'that I turned the day into such a nightmare for you.'

'Hana.' Her name sounded warm and vibrant on his lips, 'That's our work, isn't it? Yours and mine.' As he spoke he rose to his feet and came to stand in front of her so that it was impossible for her to pretend that she found the fire more fascinating. And as she raised her eyes to meet his, her hands offered themselves and he pulled her gently, firmly, inexorably to her feet. 'Besides,' he was whispering against her hair, 'it's you being here that makes it perfect. And I can't regret the events that brought you here to me. Not when they all turned out so well. Do you realise that Nicky and his foot stuck in a rock has brought us together at least a couple of months sooner that our stupid pride would have allowed.

Hana said nothing, finding perfection for the moment in lying with her ear listening to his hurrying heart, content to remain so for ever or at least until he had continued in the same vein for quite a long time. But it seemed Jake had different ideas, for with a firm finger beneath her chin he turned her face up to his, he allowed his gaze to search her features with a lazy languorous sensuality that did nothing to calm the throb of her pulses.

Then his mouth took hers and this time with none of the haste and impatience that had marked their earlier encounters. Now it was as if they had time to savour each step in their relationship, as if for the first time they could be assured that there was no need to hurry, that life and indeed love stretched invitingly ahead of them for as far as they could see.

The sensations that flowed through her body were intense and conflicting, a great easing of all the pains which had been torturing her for so long, and the blissful recognition that everything about this moment was perfect. But no matter how she imagined their feelings were under control, desire began to force aside all moderation, eacn tender exploration by his mouth, by his hands, making her more aware of her body and its intimate proximity with his. So that when at last he took his mouth from hers, held her just a little apart from him, she gave a faint moan of disappointment.

'Hana, there are things we have to say to each other. Shall we say them now, before things get out of control?' He smiled ruefully. 'I would give everything *not* to have Nicky upstairs and likely to interrupt us any moment, *not* to remember that Ted and Mary might arrive half-an-hour earlier that they said they would. If anything else happens to take you away before we have things finally worked out between us, I swear I shan't be responsible for my actions.'

So Hana found that when he subsided onto one of the huge leather chairs she was pulled down beside him, to lie against his heart, his hand holding her fast to him. And she decided that it was a tolerable position to be in. And that's what gave her the strength to tell him what she had longed to say on many occasions since that first meeting.

'I'm sorry, Jake.' It was wonderfully easy to feel free to whisper the words against his cheek, to feel the slight roughness of his beard, to wonder why that should be so wildly sensual. 'Sorry for coming here and accusing you of seducing my young nurses.'

'I suppose I ought to have been flattered. Instead all I could do was swear at Jonathan for getting me into this absurd situation, the only girl I had *really* fancied for years and all she wanted to do was tear me to shreds.'

'Was I awful?'

'Awful,' he agreed, dropping a light kiss onto the top of her head. 'And then when the next week you appeared as the new sister in Fleming . . . Well, it's hard to describe my reactions.'

'Try,' she encouraged flirtatiously.

'Well, part of me was pleased, here was this girl, the one I had had on my mind for days, and she was in a situation where she would have to jump when I snapped my fingers. It was very trying to find that I could snap as much as I liked, she just wouldn't jump.'

'You know that's not true. You were an absolute brute to me, telling me very clearly that you would neither forgive nor forget.'

'Is that the impression I made on you?' He smiled

down into her upturned face. 'Then I must have been more successful in hiding my feelings than I thought.'

'What were your feelings?' It was impossible to be serious when he had that look in his eyes.

'You know that.' His voice deepened, the smile faded from his face. 'In fact, I've told you more or less how I feel, have been feeling with increasing frustration since you arrived. What I want to know,' his arm tightened about her waist, 'is how you feel.'

'Don't you know?' she whispered as she brushed her mouth against his, 'can't you guess?'

'No,' he said huskily, 'I'm hoping, but I daren't guess. There have been so many misunderstandings between us. Tell me.' It was a command which she obeyed happily enough.

'I love you.' Then she blushed a little. 'I thought everyone in the whole hospital would know. I thought you must know.'

'Darling.' For some time there were no sounds in the room, Hana giving herself up to the dizzy delight of being held like this, being kissed like this, like nothing she had ever dreamed of.

'You don't think . . .' When a moment's sanity had returned she linked her arms, arching herself closer to his welcoming frame, '. . . that I behave like this with just *anyone*, do you?'

The moment she spoke the words, recollection of that night when James Catenby's car broke down flooded into her mind and she coloured again. 'Oh, Jake . . .' She was filled with terror lest he should doubt what she was about to say.

'What, my darling?' At the moment doubt seemed the least of his thoughts while his mouth was tracing a path of kisses from her ear towards the corner of her mouth.

'James Catenby . . .' The moment she spoke the name he paused, then held her a little apart from him.

'There's no need, you know, Hana. So long as I know it's over.'

'There's nothing to be over,' she said confusingly. 'Oh Jake, you must believe me.'

'You mean,' the dark eyes seemed suddenly to be illuminated from within, 'you mean you had decided against taking his flat.'

Hana gasped. 'How did you know?'

'Go on and tell me, Hana. Later, I'll explain what I mean.'

'James Catenby called to see me one night when his car had broken down. I *think* I saw your car fly past the gate when I was standing at the door with him.'

'Yes,' the grimness in his voice might have been a recollection of past pain, 'it was me, Hana. You'd be surprised to know how often I found a reason for travelling home by Rose Cottage.' He grinned in self-mockery, 'I must be going soft in my middle age. Probably hoped the place would be on fire so I could effect a daring rescue and that you would be so grateful that . . . But I want to hear what you have to say.'

'He had mentioned his flat before, at your party after the fête. Oh and by the way, remind me to ask you about Sagan's fortune-telling that afternoon . . .'

Jake frowned in utter, but slightly overdone perplexity, 'I can't think what you mean, my darling, but go on.'

'Well, as I said, his car broke down and he got me up out of bed to use my telephone and then he reiterated his offer of a luxury flat. He didn't mention any strings attached to his offer although I was pretty certain there would be some.'

'Mmm.' Jake frowned, 'I think we'll have to rethink Catenby's position as chairman. It's not right that he should be using his influence to suborn our nurses.'

'But, you knew about the flat!'

'Yes.' He had the grace to look just a bit sheepish, then he laughed. 'Tanya told me that you would probably be moving into the flat fairly soon. But she gave me to understand that it was simply that you could continue your relationship with more discretion. After all, who would notice Catenby's car parked outside his own block?'

'Tanya?' Hana was shocked. 'You mean to say she doesn't mind about her father behaving like that?'

'Tanya is twisted up about her father's marriage. *And* the fact that Molly provided all the money to allow him to expand at the beginning of the property boom. And I think she enjoys all the pain that Molly suffers as a result of Catenby's extra-marital activities.'

'How awful.' Hana was shocked. 'But you and she are . . .' Unable to think of a suitable description of their relationship Hana hesitated.

'Good friends?' Jake grinned down at her. 'Is that what you were about to say?'

'I . . . I don't know.' Even the thought of them being what was implied by that cliché made Hana wince.

'Can I ask you what I asked before? Are you jealous?'

'Of course I'm jealous.' To emphasise her words she beat on his chest with her fists. 'Is that what you want me to say?'

'Yes.' One strong hand captured both of hers, holding her still while his mouth whispered, 'Yes my sweet, that is exactly what I want you to say. Then perhaps you will understand how I felt when I thought you were starting an affair with James Catenby.'

'I never was, you do believe me?'

'Yes.' Tenderly he smoothed the hair back from her face, looking down into her eyes with an expression which spoke of more love than she had ever dreamed. 'What I can't believe is my own luck. Finding you. Why haven't you been snapped up years ago? Are all the young doctors blind these days?'

She shook her head, rejoicing in the soft swish of her hair, the way his eyes flicked to it then back to her face. 'Some day, I'll tell you all about it.' Briefly her mind went back to Lindsay and she realised she couldn't even remember his features. 'But now I want to ask you something.'

'Anything,' he said dangerously.

'That night, after the dance,' the recollection wasn't easy and she leaned her face against his chest, 'you told me that you'd fancied me . . .'

Jake groaned. 'You're being cruel, reminding me of what I said that night.' He sighed. 'I did apologise, you remember. I screwed up my courage,' ignoring her slight snort of disbelief he went on, 'and came along to Fleming and got no thanks for my pains. But I was sorry, I *am* sorry I said what I did. It was unforgivable. I didn't believe it at the time. It was sheer jealousy, the thought that you were using me to score off Catenby in some way. Desperate as I was to have you, I suddenly knew that I couldn't. I wanted you in love, not in some awful combination of jealousy or revenge or whatever.' He forced her chin up with one finger and looked down into her face. 'You believe me, Hana? I was angry. With you at the time, afterwards with myself.'

'Oh, Jake.' She pulled his head down to hers.

'And remember, I had been in theatre all day and half the night. I was exhausted and had a mind not to go to the dance. I knew I would want to dance with you and yet . . . I hardly dared trust myself. I thought that my control might snap. And you see, it did.' His fingers traced a tantalising path down her cheek to the corner of her mouth where they lingered, his eyes, dark and forceful, seemed to have the same interest.

'And that was when I almost blurted out the truth. That I had fancied you from the first moment I saw you. When you came quite uninvited into my life, breathing fire and indignation about my wicked ways with one of your friends.' He smiled with a touch of grimness. 'And all the time I kept thinking of what it would be like to have my wicked way with you.'

All his seriousness vanished and he was laughing down into her eyes. 'Is that what you wanted to know?'

'Yes,' she whispered, her lips moving against his.

'And,' his voice deepened suddenly, became husky and he pulled her even closer to him, 'I'll be telling you that for the rest of my life.'

In spite of herself Hana caught her breath. 'Wh . . . what do you mean?'

'What do you think I mean? I mean that you're going to marry me. Just like the gipsy foretold.'

'So it *was* you.' Indignant but pleased she flashed a reproving glance at him. 'I *knew* it must be.'

'Ssh. It's just that I know Sagan's usual spiel. It hardly varies and I honestly think she suspected. Probably noticed that when I was driving her in to work the conversation always got round to you. I can't think how I coped with work all these months. Being driven to distraction by one of the sisters is *not* conducive to good surgery.'

'Don't tell me,' her lips were brushing against his, 'that I'm the first sister who has done that.'

'You're the first for a long, long time.'

'But if even half the stories about you are true, then . . .'

'They're not, so don't let's waste time on idle speculation.'

'And Tanya?'

He gave an exaggerated sigh. 'She means nothing, although we've gone out together from time to time. While I've been waiting for you to see sense.'

'And Angie Newcombe? Are you going to tell me you haven't been making passes at her?'

'No, I'm not going to say that. So long as you admit it had the desired effect.'

'I wasn't jealous,' she lied.

'Weren't you? Then I wasted a great deal of effort. But we must get back to the most important problem.'

'And that is?' Her eyes were gleaming as she lay in his arms looking up at him.

'When are you going to stop tantalising me? How soon are you going to marry me?'

'You are sure, that what you want is . . . marriage?'

'What else had you in mind?'

'I don't know.' She blushed. 'I suppose I maybe thought . . .'

'Of course you didn't. I believe you've known for months what I was hoping for, that all this time you've simply been playing with my feelings and . . .'

'I haven't. Truly I haven't.' Their lips were touching as she spoke. 'But that night after the dance . . .'

He groaned. 'Can't we forget that? I told you, I came to the ward to apologise next day and I got a very brisk brush-off.'

'Maybe I was just thwarted. Surely you know enough about women to understand that.'

'And now,' His hands moved caressingly over her body so that she could feel their warmth even through the dressing-gown, 'will you feel thwarted tonight when you arrive back at the cottage.'

'Yes,' she whispered against his cheek, while his

mouth sought the hollows of her throat, 'Oh yes. But if you want me to stay . . .'

'Of course I want you to stay. There's nothing I want more than that. But I'm going to take you back myself. For once I have you in my bed, I'm never going to let you go again. Besides, I want our love-making to be divorced from everything that has happened today. It's all been too fraught. When you and I come together, you're going to have a ring on your finger and the marriage lines in your handbag so that I know we have all the time in the world. I think I might just be able to wait till the end of January. How does that suit you?'

'January?' Hana gasped. 'But that's much too soon and . . .'

'Well, what about St Valentine's Day. That should give you ample time to do all the things that girls have to do.' He raised an eyebrow when she began to laugh.

'I see you're going to start as you mean to continue, having your own way in everything.'

'I'm glad we understand each other.' He kissed her softly, lingeringly, so that her soft lips parted in a sigh of pleasure. 'And I promise you we shall live happily ever after, so long as you give me my own way in everything.' And to judge by the absolute silence that descended on the room, Hana could find nothing to complain of in such a promise.

Doctor Nurse Romances

Amongst the intense emotional pressures of modern medical life, doctors and nurses often find romance. Read about their lives and loves in the other three Doctor Nurse titles available this month.

TRIO OF DOCTORS
by Lindsay Hicks

'I never fall in love with nurses. They can be more dangerous than female patients.'
So Mark Barlow coolly informs Nurse Gillian Grant at their turbulent first encounter. But Gillian is in no danger of falling for the arrogant surgeon — or is she?

CASSANDRA BY CHANCE
by Betty Neels

Benedict van Manfeld, a brilliant surgeon whose sight had been severely damaged in an accident, has some excuse for his ill-temper. But is that the only reason Nurse Cassandra Darling continues to put up with his ranting and raging?

AUSTRIAN INTERLUDE
by Lee Stafford

Melody Cameron finds a happiness she had never dreamed of when she takes on a private nursing assignment near the beautiful Austrian city of Salzburg. But can her feelings for Dr Dieter von Rheinhof bring her anything more than heartache?

Mills & Boon
the rose of romance

How to join in a whole new world of romance

It's very easy to subscribe to the Mills & Boon Reader Service. As a regular reader, you can enjoy a whole range of special benefits. Bargain offers. Big cash savings. Your own free Reader Service newsletter, packed with knitting patterns, recipes, competitions, and exclusive book offers.

We send you the very latest titles each month, postage and packing free – no hidden extra charges. There's absolutely no commitment – you receive books for only as long as you want.

We'll send you details. Simply send the coupon – or drop us a line for details about the Mills & Boon Reader Service Subscription Scheme. Post to: Mills & Boon Reader Service, P.O. Box 236, Thornton Road, Croydon, Surrey CR9 3RU, England. *Please note: READERS IN SOUTH AFRICA please write to: Mills & Boon Reader Service of Southern Africa, Private Bag X3010, Randburg 2125, S. Africa.

Please send me details of the Mills & Boon Subscription Scheme.

NAME (Mrs/Miss) _____ EP3

ADDRESS _____

_____

COUNTY/COUNTRY_____ POST/ZIP CODE_____

BLOCK LETTERS, PLEASE

Mills & Boon
the rose of romance